Love in Mission City: The Shorts

Page Against the Machine

The Lightkeeper's Love Affair

Not in it for the Money

Marcus's Cadence

Ace's Place

Cover art by Jo Clement

Edits by ELF

Contents

Introduction

L ove in Mission City: The Shorts Box Set includes one novellas and four short stories that have been previously published

Mission City is tucked in the charming Cedar Valley in southwestern British Columbia. If you love heartwarming, contemporary small-town gay romances, then come home to Mission City and fall in love with the men who live there. Romance blossoms in the unlikeliest places. And trouble has a way of finding them...

Page Against the Machine

Dickens has run his family bookstore for years in the quiet ambiance suitable for literary endeavors. When Spike opens a motorcycle repair shop next door, tempers flare and sparks fly. Will they be able to resolve their differences or are they just too stubborn for compromise?

This is a 25k sizzling gay romance novella with a true instalove, enemies to lovers, opposites attract story with a cuddly cat named Aristotle.

The Lightkeeper's Love Affair

Ben's graduation celebration is disrupted by a winter storm. He and his beagle, Buddy, have the only room left in the hotel. When lightkeeper Isaac needs a bed, though, Ben's happy to share. Platonically, of course. Except something about Isaac makes Ben want more.

This is a 10k lighthearted gay romance with forced proximity, a loner, a future school-teacher, and Buddy, the adorable beagle.

Marcus's Cadence

Cadence is trying to sell the home that had been his refuge during his tumultuous teen years. When his teenage crush, Marcus, shows up as a potential buyer, sparks fly. Is there just a real estate deal to be done or could his feelings be requited? (You don't want to imply sex/love is part of a deal)

This is a 7k second-chance gay romance instalove short story with a very happy ending and a malti-poo named Kiki.

Not in it for the Money

August's beloved sister has passed suddenly and the man finds himself in need of comfort. Turning to his employee feels all kinds of wrong, but Julian's arms feel too damned right to resist. Come morning, though, they have to look reality in the face. Is there a chance they find a forever love out of the tragedy?

This is a 5k scorching gay romance story about a boss, his employee, and the inheritance of a lifetime.

Ace's Place

After a fall from grace, Derek has moved to a small town for a fresh start. Harold, the local golden boy made good, catches Derek's attention. But secrets and omissions cloud what could be the beginning of something special. Can they take a chance on being vulnerable enough to fall in love?

This is a 13k steamy gay romance about second-chances, hockey, and an adorable but nosy Bouvier.

Page Against the Machine

A Mission City Gay Romance Novella

Gabbi Grey

Dickens

My tranquility is shattered when a motorcycle repair shop moves in next to my bookstore. All I want is peace and quiet. What I get is gunning engines and eighties rock music. One of us has got to go, and since I was here first, it's the hot mechanic.

Spike

I chose Mission City to set up shop because of the weekend-enthusiast riders. I've dreamed of owning my own shop for years, and no one is going to run me out of town. Least of all the adorable geek Bookstore Dude.

This 25k gay romance novella is a true instalove, enemies to lovers, opposites attract story with a cuddly cat named Aristotle. The story first appeared in the anthology Love Is All Volume 5.

Dedication

Wendy, Jeanine, and Renae

Contents

Chapter One

Dickens

"One caramel macchiato extra hot." Sunshine put the cup on the counter in front of me.

I'd been so absorbed in the ordering system, I hadn't heard her come in. I scowled.

"The bell above the door is working fine, boss." She tapped my forehead above my frown. "You're too focused on placing the next order." She glanced over at the screen. "That's not enough."

My scowl deepened. "I don't want to end up with extra inventory."

"And the last time she released a book, we sold out in two hours and had customers complaining for days while we tried to secure more copies. She's taken off since then. Hometown girl made good." She tucked a strand of her blue-black hair behind her ears and her pale-blue eyes shone. "You should triple that order. I'm telling you—Raven's new book is going to be a bestseller. Plus, you can do more online orders if you've got extra." She tapped her neat, polish-free finger on the counter. "But we're not going to have surplus stock."

I tried to argue with her logic, but, as always, her reasoning was sound. "Have you asked her about doing a signing?"

"Boss, you know her as well as I do. And you're the owner of the store."

"Didn't you say your sister went to school with her?"

Sun rolled her eyes. "Yes, Rainbow was in Raven's class. Yes, she used to hang out at our place. But you're the proprietor of this establishment." She waved her hand around. "I'm just the employee."

My scowl returned with a vengeance. "Bullshit."

She tisked.

"Oh, please. There's no one here."

One perfect eyebrow arched.

Damn, if she'd come in without me hearing her, then...

"Relax." Her grin split her face. "No one else is here, so take a breath. And fine, I'll call Raven. I'm assuming you want her to do a reading as well? I'll see if she's available for an evening or weekend presentation. She teaches university during the day, and her books are young adult, so we want the kids to be able to attend."

"You know a huge percentage of young-adult fiction readers are actually adults."

"I was aware of that." Her eyes flashed.

"Of course you were."

Sunshine had been an employee of the bookstore for over ten years. She started when my parents still owned the store and had fortunately stayed on after they retired and turned the store over to me. My folks were happily enjoying their time up in the Okanagan region of British Columbia while The Owl's Nest bookstore they founded sat in Mission City, part of the tranquil Fraser Valley. We were within spitting distance of Vancouver, but we retained a small-town feeling.

"I'm going to open the box we got yesterday and—"

"It's already done."

Now she scowled.

I shrugged. "I was bored."

"Boss." No missing the exasperated tone. "When your parents renovated the second floor and turned it into an apartment for you, I'm positive they didn't intend for you to spend all your spare time in the store."

I'd concede that much. They hadn't wanted me worrying about a mortgage. Their ingenuity meant I had a lovely home above the shop. It also meant I could come down whenever I had insomnia. The smell of books invariably soothed me, and I'd soon be ready to crawl back into bed. "Well, I'm sure you can find—"

The sound of a gunshot rang through the store.

My first instinct was to duck, but gunfire in Mission City was ridiculous. Ah, must be a car backfiring. "So if—"

Another one.

My gaze shot to Sunshine.

She raised an eyebrow as if to say, *what's your point*?

This time, a motor revved.

My hackles rose.

"Drink your coffee, boss. I have some news." She inclined her head. "Remember when the McKinneys sold their store?"

"Sure. About six months ago." Where was she going with this?

"And you didn't know who bought it?"

"I presume you're going to enlighten me?" I loved her, but occasionally she took her sweet time getting to the point.

"A motorcycle repair shop."

I gaped. "How did they move in and I didn't notice?"

She rolled her eyes. "You just spent the last week at a book-buying convention in New Orleans, and you stopped in New York and Chicago. Did you think the world held its breath while you were gone?"

"Well, frankly, yes. This is Mission City. Nothing ever happens in Mission—"

Another loud rev.

"Goddamnit."

She snickered. "Whatever." She waved her hand. "They had a crew come in last week. Pretty much worked twenty-four/seven. Got the entire thing done up. Looks pretty spiffy. Of course, in a week or two, there'll be a layer of grease and—"

"They can't stay." I pushed my glasses up my nose. "Absolutely not. We can't have a repair shop next to the bookstore. Oh, why did the McKinneys have to sell?"

"Because they literally won the lottery?" She snorted. "And moved back to Prince Edward Island to be with their kids. Why run a hardware store when you can sit and watch the ocean waves?"

"I..." I had no idea. Not about any of it. I worked. I worked hard. I couldn't fathom sitting around all day looking at water. No, my parents gave me a job when I was thirteen, and I'd worked almost every day since—when I wasn't in school. So, in other words, half my life.

This tangent was getting me nowhere.

Another rumble.

I flailed my arms at the huge overstuffed chairs. "We want readers to come in, put their feet up, and stay awhile. How're they going to be able to think, let alone concentrate on a book, with all that racket?" I pounded my fist on the counter, startling us both. "I'm going over there."

She giggle-snorted. "To do what? They have as much right to be here as we do."

"No. We were here first. Downtown Mission City doesn't need that...noise." Could I add more derision to the word? Possibly. Nah, probably not.

Sun placed a hand over my fist. Instantly, a wave of calm washed over me.

Damn woman. I wanted to be mad, and she wanted me to be placid. Sometimes, her sensitive nature overwhelmed my swirling emotions. She often brought peace when my mind spiraled into chaos. On the flip side, I possessed a drive she didn't have within her. Synergism. I managed the business side, and she handled customers. We could change lanes when we needed to. But why mess with something that worked so well?

And the woman's sensitivities sometimes veered into psychic abilities, but we never talked about that.

"He's a nice man. You don't need to go over there all upset and make a fuss." She stroked her finger along my thumb. "You need to go and introduce yourself. Welcome him to the neighborhood. I won't say too much, but—" She glanced around, letting me know she was about to impart a great secret. "—he's lonely."

"So what?" I almost said I was lonely, and it was no big deal, but being that personal with my employee didn't seem a good idea. The sympathy in those sky-blue eyes assured me that my unspoken comment had also been understood. "Fine, I'll be nice." Grudging.

"Take him a black coffee."

I arched a brow.

"A hunch."

No point arguing or snickering. I grabbed my formerly extra-hot drink and headed out into the morning sun.

Our store faced south, so we had sun for a good part of the day. The sun blazed overhead, promising another scorcher. Mid-June, and we'd already set record temperatures for most of the spring. And really dry too, which meant my parents were likely to have to endure smoke from the wildfires.

I'd tried to dissuade them from heading up into the interior, but they'd tired of *city* living. I missed them.

I pivoted away from the new store and headed down the road to Tim Horton's. No line-up this morning, so I secured a cup of dark roast and a six-pack of Timbits. Nothing said gracious more than offering half-a-dozen donut holes.

As I wandered back past my shop, I snuck a peek into the front window.

Aristotle lay resplendent in her window seat, perched upon her preferred pillow. She was a favorite amongst all the patrons, although she was getting older. Still, she was as cute as the day I brought her home.

I'd heard about a litter of kittens found abandoned by the railway tracks.

They'd been in rough shape, and the littlest one had a broken leg, some nasty bites, and an infection.

Sunshine's older sister, Dr. Zephyra Dixon, had stepped up to offer her veterinary skills for free.

The deal was, I could keep one of the kittens if I raised enough money to pay for the medicines they required. Being all of fifteen, I organized a bake sale at school and guilted everyone I knew into baking and then goaded them into buying the sometimes-questionable results. I raised enough to cover the costs for all the kittens. To my pride and joy, all found good homes. I got my pick of the litter and, of course, chose the little black-and-white one.

After recovering from her broken leg, Ari thrived under the love.

I begged my parents to bring her to the shop so she wouldn't be alone all day.

They rolled their eyes, but did as I requested and, for all those years, they hauled that cat home every night and back to the store every morning.

When I moved in upstairs, she naturally followed me home every night.

Sunshine watched her while I was out of town.

She opened her eyes, blinked lazily in the sunlight, licked her paw, and then laid her head back down on the pillow.

I wouldn't have her with me forever, of course, but I'd enjoy every minute until the time came.

Another engine blast raked across my nerves.

Determinedly, I stalked over to the store.

Spike's Cycles' façade was much the same as it'd been when the McKinneys owned it. Brown brick with a huge plate-glass window. The old-fashioned wood door had been replaced with a metal one, and the gray color stuck out as too modern.

Oh well.

I opened the door and stepped inside.

The waiting room had three metal chairs, a coffee table with some magazines, and a counter. A couple motorcycle posters adorned the wall.

The room felt jarringly new, but that'd soon dissipate, I was sure. I tried to see past the counter into the back room, but spotted nothing. I exited the store and headed around the corner.

They'd partitioned part of the old parking lot with high wire fencing and razor wire at the top.

It stood out like the proverbial sore thumb and didn't fit with the aesthetic of First Avenue.

Well, maybe it matched the car dealership at the other end of the street, but that'd been there as long as I could remember.

An overhang covered much of the space, but part of the brick had been torn away to create a massive rolling door that sat open. Three motorcycles sat on the asphalt. No, wait, a fourth sporty type one sat off to the side. Lime green.

Oh, Lord.

The sun glinted off the chrome, nearly blinding me. I squinted and, finally, spotted a human being. He knelt on some kind of mat, giving me the most wonderful view of his amazing ass. His jeans fit like a second skin, and his jean shirt did nothing to hide his broad expanse of back and muscled arms.

He pulled something, and as he shifted, he dropped the wrench.

"Fuck."

I cleared my throat.

His body twisted as he reacted to my voice and he nearly knocked the bike over. He righted it. Then he righted himself as he rose. He turned and glared. "Don't you know not to creep up on a guy?"

Creep up on? I pointed to the store. "I tried going in there first."

The scowl didn't lighten, but he did shrug. "Okay, what do you have?"

"Have?"

Oh.

I held out the coffee and Timbits. "Just welcoming you to the neighborhood."

He hesitated.

Far too long. God, did he think I poisoned it or something?

Finally, at length, he wiped his brow with a rag and removed his sunglasses.

Wow. Just wow. Eyes the same dark brown as my ex-boyfriend's. His hair was as dark as Sunshine's, although with hints of light brown in the bright sunlight. He had a beard. Not a full beard, but a nice version of trimmed scruff.

I held up the coffee, and he finally accepted it.

"Uh, thank you."

"My pleasure." And it would be, if I got to look at this guy all the time.

He was my every fantasy come to life.

Chapter Two

Spike

With great reluctance, I took the offered coffee and the little box of Timbits. Yum, my favorites. But I wasn't going to let this guy see that. I couldn't put my finger on why, but my hackles rose at him. Something about his friendly greeting rang hollow. And with the fancy button-down shirt, pressed khaki slacks, and...oh my God, were those loafers? Even his glasses screamed geek. Now, I wasn't one to pass judgement. Geeks owned motorcycles, too. Well, I'd known a couple. Um, yeah, one. Marvin—the accountant who did my taxes back in Surrey. Most of the guys I was used to dealing with were biker dudes. We'd operated in that part of town.

But here? In Mission City? I hoped to cater to a different clientele. Enthusiasts who rode for fun.

This guy? Discomfort radiated off of him. Probably thought the grease would magically leap from my hands to his pristine clothes. As I sipped the black coffee he brought—my favorite—I scrutinized his dirty-blond, close-cropped, slightly spikey hair and those dark-blue eyes virtually hidden behind the black, plastic-framed glasses. "Well, thank you for the welcome."

He continued to watch me intently.

Heat rose in my cheeks and I tried to hold his stare. Something about this guy irked me, but what? His welcome to the neighborhood didn't ring true. The coffee and Timbits were nice, but this didn't feel like a genuine reception. "You haven't told me your name."

He fluttered his hand through his hair.

Ha, so not unaffected.

"Dickens."

"Yeah, okay, but what's your first name?"

"Dickens." With a slight bite.

Ah, so a little touchy about his name. I could relate. I took another sip.

"And *your* name?" Another slight bite.

"It's on the front door."

His brows shot up. "Your name is Spike? That a family name?"

I crossed my arms.

He took a step back.

Well, that was easy. Except, did I want him to back up? The guy was fucking gorgeous, and the more time I spent looking at his lips, the more I wanted to know if they were as soft as they appeared. I wanted to rub myself against him to see if he was as supple as he looked. I wanted to grind my cock into his to see if we could generate some friction.

"Sure, Spike's a family name. Whatever." Of course it wasn't, and we both knew it. But I wasn't admitting my true first name to anyone in the world. And if my mother hadn't chosen it, I'd have changed it years ago. But it felt wrong to want to dump something she'd selected with loving care. Even if it had been the source of never-ending bullying and torment for most of my life. Someone at the old shop said I was as spikey as a hedgehog. I later learned the expression was prickly, but spikey caught on, and soon everyone called me Spike. It stuck. So when I struck out on my own, it made sense to keep the name.

"Yes, well, as you say." He ran his hand through his hair again. The strands were becoming as spikey as my name. "I just...do you think...?" He faltered visibly.

"Spit it out, man. I don't have all day." Despite having just opened officially this morning—to exactly zero fanfare—I already had three machines to work on, plus my own beauty needed a tune-up. I'd racked up quite a few miles, coming back and forth between Surrey and my new place. Movers delivered everything Friday, and now, Monday morning, I was set and ready to go.

"I..." He took a deep breath. "I'm wondering if you could keep the noise down?"

I blinked. "Come again?"

"Well, you know, we like a peaceful downtown, and your, uh, bikes are very loud."

He was serious? "Look, Dickens, I don't know what you're talking about. People drive down First Avenue all the time. And there's parking on the street. Also, in case you haven't noticed, the train whistles go off all the time."

Now he blinked. "They're part of the fabric of our town and its history. We've always had industries that rely on the railway. And the commuter train, of course."

"Of course." I scrunched my nose. "So all that noise is okay, but not the occasional motorcycle engine."

His spine visibly stiffened as he stood straighter. "Occasional? It's been revving all morning. And those things—" He pointed with obvious disdain, "—are designed to be a menace. People make them deliberately louder than they need to be just so they can disrupt the peace."

Well, I couldn't argue with that. Did I encourage people to do that? Of course not. If they wanted it, did I dissuade them? No to that as well. "I haven't been revving anything all morning. I needed to check out this baby's carburetor to make sure she was working properly." I pointed to the Kawasaki. "That one's next."

He took a sip of his drink and scowled.

"Problem?"

"It's cold."

Ah. Mr. Prissy didn't like cold coffee either. Well, if he hadn't stood around whining, it wouldn't have grown cold. I, however, was not going to point that out. "Look, buddy, I have to get back to work. I'll try not to be too loud." Totally impossible promise to make, but I really wanted him to take his uptight ass off my property and back to wherever he'd come from. "Hey, where do you work?"

"The Owl's Nest."

The...? Oh, right, the shop next door. The one with books all over the front window. "That's a bookshop, right?"

"Of course."

Guy actually rolled his eyes. I couldn't think of him as Dickens. The name was just too pretentious. Well, on the other hand, it suited him. But I didn't want to think about Dickens because that'd remind me of my mom, and I so didn't want to go down that particular path. "Well, head on back to your bookshop. I have work to do."

He harrumphed.

Actually harrumphed.

Then he pivoted and stomped out of sight.

Except loafers on the cement sidewalk didn't have the same effect as, for example, high heels clacking on hardwood. He reminded me of my old boss, Gia. She'd inherited the shop when she was barely twenty-two. Her old man passed suddenly of a heart attack at age fifty. She shucked the biker-babe persona and became a businesswoman. She ran a tight ship and there'd been no bullshit around her place.

All that being said, she loved her high heels and short skirts. She remarried a year ago to my accountant. He brought his bike in for a tune-up, and she strutted out of the office on those spikey heels and, voilà—as my mom would say—they hit it off and three weeks later wore matching leather bike outfits to Surrey City Hall and got married. Gia didn't mellow and Marvin didn't swagger, but they did all right.

I had Gia's unconditional support to start my own place. Fifteen years I worked in her shop. Fifteen years of scrimping and saving every dime so I could build something from the ground up.

So how dare he? How fucking dare he come by and ask me to keep the noise down? Really? People drove down First Avenue, and they weren't quiet. More than a few motorcycles passed by—one of the reasons I knew this location was perfect. Trains went by all day and night. They rumbled and blew their whistles. More than once the past few nights I'd awoken to the sound. It'd take getting used to.

Just like fucking Dickens would get used to my revving engines on occasion. Wasn't like I was doing it to intentionally irritate him.

Tempting as that might be.

I washed my hands and then dug into the box of Timbits, demolishing all but the birthday cake one with sparkles. I'd save that for dessert. I eyed the Harley with a mixture of frustration and envy. She was a beauty, but she was being a beast.

Time to tame her.

And put the gorgeous, blue-eyed blond out of my mind.

Or at least try to.

Chapter Three

Dickens

"What kind of a name is Spike?" Not that I'd spent most of the day obsessing over the hot new neighbor.

Sunshine gave me a long, level look.

"Well?"

Slowly, she smiled.

Seriously? "What are you smiling about?"

She quirked an eyebrow. "I think you like him."

"Preposterous."

"And I think he likes you."

"Sun, you haven't even met the guy."

"Who says?"

My brain screeched to a halt like a needle scratching a record. "What?"

"You think I didn't go next door to introduce myself and welcome him to town?"

She smiled that serene smile that always drove me nuts. Like she knew something I didn't and wasn't likely to share. "And?" A demand she wasn't likely to obey.

"His name isn't really Spike." She held up her hand to ward off my questions. "But he didn't share his birth name, and I didn't push. He's been a mechanic for fifteen years, used to work in a shop in Surrey, and recently crossed the Fraser River to take up residence in our fair city." She tapped a finger to her lips. "And you guys are more alike than you think."

Was she...?

Her eyes sparkled. "And no, he didn't tell me that either. Tries to keep it hidden, so respect that. Not all guys are out and proud like yourself."

She didn't need to mention I hadn't always been. My parents paid for me to attend the University of British Columbia in Vancouver to study business administration.

Sure, I could've commuted every day, but they wanted me to have the full college experience, so I'd lived in a dorm for those four years. And experimented. Plenty. By the time I turned twenty-two and was ready to graduate, I felt comfortable coming out to my parents.

And since Sunshine was like a member of the family, she was looped in.

My parents were, of course, incredibly supportive. Possibly a little miffed it took me so long to come out, because they'd suspected since I was in my early teens.

Sun had been sure, of course, but hadn't breathed a word.

"Slim pickings these days." Sure, gay guys lived in Mission City. I even knew a few, including a realtor and a counselor up at Sunshine's sister Kennedy's counseling center. Cadence and Justin were nice guys. They were also...not my type.

Both were around my age, both were very handsome, and both were very much tops.

And since I was as well, the compatibility hadn't been there. Had I been tempted? Sure. But why start a relationship knowing certain things would never work?

"Well, your perfect companion is right next door."

"Sun." I injected as much menace and warning as I could into my voice and her response was, of course, to laugh.

"I'm finished for the day." She leaned down to scoop Ari into her arms.

The cat purred and head-butted her neck.

"Want to come home with me? I'll miss you."

Sun had kept Ari for the past week, but I'd missed my little one. Well, at nearly twenty pounds, she wasn't that little. Once, I could hold her in the palm of my hand. Not so much these days.

My errant employee dropped said deadweight onto the counter, and Ari immediately bolted for the keyboard.

I held it up and away, but it was a near thing.

Sunshine laughed all the way out of the store.

Crazy woman. How she could be so happy, given her nine-month marriage ended last month, was beyond me. Or maybe that's why she was happy. I liked Colton Pritchard just fine, but he wasn't the right man for Sun. The serious RCMP officer had recently been promoted to a corporal in sex crimes.

Sun was a woman who radiated warmth and goodness.

I think she believed she could lighten up the man.

Well, it hadn't worked. Now she was alone again. Barely twenty-seven, and two disastrous marriages she needed to put in the rearview mirror.

She had shadows, of course.

Logan, her first husband, had been a stand-up guy. Lots of fun. Then he joined the army, and after a harrowing overseas deployment, had come home a different man.

She tried to buoy him, but he'd wound up taking a swing at her.

He'd left, and despite my general empathy for those serving our country, I'd been happy to see his ass departing.

Then she married Colton before the ink was barely dry on her divorce. Another dark man. She had a type, and it didn't suit her.

Was Spike my type? Sun knew my preferences, of course. We'd had a way-too-frank discussion not long after I came out. She'd been curious, and I'd just broken up with a guy because of our sexual incompatibility. I would've loved to blame it on booze or pot or some other mind-altering substance. The truth? My heart had broken. I really loved Isaac. My first, and if I'd had my way, my only.

Alas, after our experimentation phase ended, we discovered a lack of compatibility. That and he had to go back to Whitehorse when he graduated, and no way was I moving to the Yukon. So I came home to Mission City with the focus of taking over my parents' shop and the vain hope of putting Sunshine in her place.

I'd succeeded in one of those things.

Ari sat on the counter and blinked lazy eyes up at me.

"No, you're not getting treats."

Another blink.

"All right. But just one. Dr. Zephyra said you're a little heavy, and it's hard on your joints."

My cat could probably care less about what her beloved vet's pronouncements were. With more care than she deserved, I picked her up and set her down on the floor. I meandered through the store to ensure everything was straight. Of course Sunshine had likely just done the same thing, so everything was perfect.

I flipped the sign on the door, flicked the lock, and lowered the blinds. Mission City wasn't a high-crime area, but having the cash register visible from the street wasn't a great idea. I put the cash away in the floor safe in the back room, then encouraged Ari to head up the stairs. I set the alarm for the store, then closed that door and headed upstairs.

My cat made a beeline for her food bowl and glared up at me.

"I know Sun fed you this morning, so don't try to tell me you're hard done by. I won't believe you."

Still, I located some of her favorite expensive kibble and scooped out the appropriate portion. I opened my fridge and surveyed the contents. I'd been a responsible adult and had stopped at the grocery store on my way back into town last night, even though I'd been tired.

Was I up to cooking or—

All logical thought fled as the most horrendous racket thundered through my apartment. Only the steady bass assured me that I wasn't enduring an earthquake. Nothing shook, but Ari looked up from her bowl and gave me a *what the fuck* look. This was bad. Anything that separated my cat from her food was a pretty dire thing.

Locating the source of the noise wasn't a challenge. My kitchen shared a wall with Spike's new place.

The McKinneys had used the loft as a storage space.

Apparently Spike was either using it as an office or—God forbid—an apartment. Oh shit. Bad enough I had to deal with his noise shit during the day. But at night? I was accustomed to quiet.

Aside from the occasional train whistle, downtown Mission City was tranquil. Even Tim Horton's and the Greek restaurant—Stavros's—closed up before eleven. Occasionally a truck rumbled through, but those were few and far between.

My peace was shattered, and I was pissed.

Ari still gazed up at me.

Appease her.

I snagged a tin of wet food and apportioned a slice on a plate for her.

She eyed it greedily as I placed the plate on the floor, but she waited for me to give her permission before she dug in.

Satisfied she'd be okay, I tromped down the stairs. I exited through the back door and stomped over to the next building. The back of our stores faced a back alley, and I had two parking spaces. I kept my Prius in one, and Sunshine used the other when she drove to work.

Spike's parking space was filled with a beat-up pickup truck that'd seen better days. The windows facing the alley were all shut.

I, on the other hand, had all mine open. I had a/c but used it infrequently, preferring the breeze off the river. On the days when the wind didn't blow, and the temperatures climbed to over one hundred, I broke down and cranked her up. Naturally we used a/c in the store. Wouldn't do to have our guests sweating to death.

The closed windows and the still-thumping bass assured me I'd never be heard. I circled around to the front of the store. The noise wasn't so insane out here, but I could still hear it.

Most of the stores didn't have apartments over top, and many of the shops were shuttered for the night.

Still, this was rude.

I pounded on the door.

Unsurprisingly, nothing happened. I glanced around.

The main street was, surprisingly, empty.

"Hey, asshole."

"I hope you're not referring to me."

I spun and my stomach sank.

Corporal Colton Pritchard from the RCMP stood across the road from me in the shadow of the storefront for the cell phone repair shop.

Damn.

Sunshine's asshole ex-husband.

Well, not exactly an asshole. Not a bad guy. Just not suited to my favorite employee and good friend.

The polite thing to do would be to cross the street so I wasn't yelling. I checked traffic and hustled across First Avenue. "Uh, everything's fine." I cleared my throat. "Lovely night. Are you, uh, alone?"

He pointed down the street. "Dorrie and I just got off shift and decided to grab Tim Horton's. I thought I'd wander down this way. I miss patrol duty."

Well, that didn't sit right with me. He'd hated patrol duty, and that was why he'd pushed for the job in special victims—a promotion and a way off the streets.

Was it possible he was staking out the bookstore? Checking to see if Sunshine was still around? "She's gone home."

"I wasn't..." The unflappable cop's expression darkened.

Oh yeah, he was.

He was also out of uniform and looking like an ordinary civilian. Albeit one who topped six feet by a couple of inches. He towered over me. And while I was lean and wiry, he was buff and cut.

Movement caught my eye, and I spotted Dorrie Duhamel making her way down the street carrying a Tim Horton's paper bag and a tray with two paper cups. At least that part of the story wasn't a lie. Why here? At this moment? Three guesses and the first two didn't count.

"Hey, Dorrie." We'd gone to school together, but while she'd studied criminology at the Justice Institute, I'd headed into business. She didn't look any more comfortable than I felt.

"Everything okay, Dickens?

Her question refocused me. "I was knocking on my neighbor's door to ask him to turn down the music."

She cocked her head.

"Well, it's much louder inside. It's reverberating through my entire apartment and it's disrupting Ari while she's eating."

Dorrie handed the tray to Colton. She snagged a cup for herself and took a sip. "How is Aristotle these days? I haven't dropped in recently."

I eyed Colton. Yeah, it'd be awkward to have his partner visit while the guy's ex-wife was working. Dorrie and Sunshine had been close. How had this split affected their friendship? "I'll let you guys get on with..." I waved my hand in the general direction of their food.

"You want me to talk to him?" Dorrie's blue eyes softened on me. "For Ari's sake?"

Oh God, I was so pathetic. "No, that's okay. I can, you know, use earplugs or something."

Colton's dark gaze pierced me. "That's no way to live. Let us talk to him."

And have him know I sicced the cops on him his first week in town? No way.

I ran my hand through my hair. "I'm good. Really good. I'll just leave you to your, uh, dinner." I pivoted, waited for two cars to pass, then trotted across the street.

Jaywalking.

Jesus.

I strode around to the back of our properties. I could throw rocks at the window, but if one broke, I'd be in deep shit. Finally, defeated, I re-entered the building and headed back upstairs.

Ari awaited me with a *what the fuck* expression still in her deep-amber eyes.

I inched over to the front windows and crooked a finger to pull back the drapes to see out. I kept them closed on hot days because of the afternoon sun, but I threw them open at night to let in the cool night air.

Dorrie and Colton sat on a bench across the street, eating their sandwiches.

Did she not think it odd they sat in front of the store where his ex-wife worked? I was pretty sure nothing was going on between the two of them, but I'd been wrong before. Not about Sunshine and Colton, though. That marriage had been doomed from the start.

Should I call Sunshine to tell her—

Jesus Fucking Christ. Was he playing...Whitesnake? *Here I Go Again*. An eighties hair band? Seriously? I wanted to pound on the wall, but even I wasn't that stupid. Solid brick. Should've been enough to keep out the noise.

I stalked to the bedroom to nab my iPod. I selected an audiobook and turned it on full volume.

And winced. I didn't want to sacrifice my hearing just to block out the noise. Still, it lowered the rock music to a dull roar, and as I prepared my dinner, I tried not to cringe. No way was I going to be able to live like this for the next fifty years.

Hell, I'd be lucky to make it to the end of the week.

Chapter Four

Spike

Contrary to the image of biker dudes who drank beer and shot pool all night, I was an early riser. Nothing I loved more than heading out onto the open road and watching the sun rise. Tuesday morning, I did just that. Followed Railway Avenue to where it joined the Number Seven and rode right out of town toward Deroche. I wanted to go up to Agassiz or Hope, but I had to be responsible and open the store at nine-thirty. Unlikely anyone would notice if I was later, but I'd know. Responsible business owner.

Scared shitless.

I had a stack of paperwork I ignored last night as I painted my living room. In hindsight, I should've opened the windows sooner, but the day'd been hot and my a/c kept my place cool. Plus I blared my music pretty loud, and I didn't want people meandering down First Avenue to hear my eclectic choices. No, better to keep all that to myself.

The sun glittered across the Fraser River as I drove down the winding road. My sunglasses dulled most of the glare, and despite having my helmet on, the wind whipped through my hair as I'd left it loose. I wanted to floor it, but traffic was getting heavier. With reluctance, I turned back at the dike. More cars surrounded me as I made my way westward.

A few of these insane souls made the drive to Mission City every morning before either hopping onto the commuter train or—if they were really nuts—driving the rest of the way to Vancouver.

As the Mission City sign greeted me, I soaked in the welcome implicit in the greeting. I'd made the right choice, coming out here.

Plus, real estate was half the cost of Vancouver's. Creeping up with stunning velocity, but still cheaper for now. Even less than Surrey.

No, small town living suited me. I'd come from Kitimat, a small town up the coast toward Alaska. I'd blown town the moment I turned eighteen and hadn't looked back. My father hadn't asked me where I was going, and I'd never written to let him know.

I slowed down at the sign for thirty kilometers per hour through this main part of downtown Mission City. The street ran one way, and I eyed the Tim Horton's. Better not. Until I had a steadier clientele, I couldn't afford to eat too many meals out.

I'd taught myself to cook more than just KD and ramen noodles, so I had plenty of healthy foods in my fridge. A quick omelet before I started the day would hit the spot. Maybe a piece of toast with peanut butter and blueberry jam. I parked the bike by the front gate, hopped off, opened the gate, then drove through. I shut off the engine and was making my way back over to the gate, intending to lock it until opening time, when a blur of movement caught my eye.

Bookstore Dude strode into my yard, arms gesticulating. He was shouting something, but I couldn't make out the words. I held up my hand, and he halted. I removed my sunglasses and helmet. As I shook out my hair, I asked, "What are you blathering on about?"

A vein in his neck pulsed and his cheeks were hectic with color. His hair looked extra spikey, as it he'd been running his hands through it. "I said, 'what the fuck is wrong with you?' "

The words came out venomous, and I gaped. "What are you talking about?"

He waved wildly. "You play that god-awful music half the night, and then you're up before the ass crack of dawn, gunning your engine and taking off to God knows where—"

"Deroche."

"Deroche," he repeated. His face contorted into a weird look of disgust. "You got up at that hour to go to Deroche? Why, for God's sake?"

"You're taking the Lord's name in vain quite a bit this morning." Former Christian who attended the church from the moment I was born until the moment I told them I was gay. Let's just say the Lord and I parted ways after that clusterfuck.

He chuffed. "Apologies to your moral sensibilities. Why..." He floundered. "Why Deroche?"

"Because then I was driving into the sun. Lovely morning, and I wanted to get a ride in before the day started. Responsible entrepreneur and all that." I removed my leather jacket. The sun was high and climbing higher by the minute. Another scorcher.

"Well, I barely got any sleep." His scowl was both deep and sexy.

"Yeah, you said something about music?"

"Your horrendous music. You played it so loud and—"

I held up my hand. "You're saying you can hear it through the brick wall?"

"Yes, I'm saying I can hear it through the brick wall." He wagged his finger at me. Actually wagged his finger at me. "I wanted peace and quiet, and I got Aerosmith."

"I'm surprised a young one such as yourself would even recognize eighties music."

"I'm twenty-seven years old, for fuck's sake."

"You're kind of making my point. Millennial."

He scowled. "What are you, a Boomer?"

This guy was way too smart for that comment not to be sarcasm. "I'm a late Generation X."

"You're not that old."

Damn cocky, this one. "Maybe not, but I feel that old." I did. I was also a Millennial, but I straddled the line. Most days I felt old. Not wise. Just old.

He waved me off. "What does this have to do with respecting your neighbor?"

"Look, I didn't know you could hear the music. I'll keep it down from now on." I yanked my keys from my pocket and moved to the side door to my shop. I figured he'd take the hint, and once he disappeared, I'd go back out and lock the gate. I strode into the store and was hanging my jacket on the peg when I realized he followed me.

He slammed the door.

Then he had the temerity to wag his finger in my face. Swear to God, I was within a breath of breaking the fucking thing. "What do you want now? I told you I'd keep the music down."

"And what about taking your motorcycle out at five in the morning?"

"Doesn't the train leave the station at five-thirty? I've heard the bells at that hour." Drove me nuts the first few days, but I got used to it. Just like Bookstore Dude would get used to hearing me drive away. "And, for the record, my bike isn't that loud."

He grunted.

That sound shot right through me and straight into my cock. I growled.

He took a step back. Then he cocked his head.

The moment spun out until understanding dawned.

"Fuck me." His words whispered across the space.

"Well, frankly, I'd prefer you fuck me." I started to tug my hair so I could tie it. "If it's all the same with you."

"Leave your hair down."

My hand stilled.

"I'm going to yank it while I pound into you. I'm going to make you fucking scream."

Okay, then.

To be clear, I was completely onboard with this notion. I'd wanted him since the moment I spotted him yesterday, and the less-than-subtle hints Sunshine had fed me over the past week assured me we'd be compatible. In passing, I wondered just how much this dude shared with his employee, but part of me also sensed she was determining my suitability as a match. Well, she hadn't been wrong. We were going to be a good match.

In bed, at least.

Except there wasn't one in sight, and I wasn't sure I wanted to drag him up to my apartment. Not only was the place a disaster area, but that felt too personal. This wasn't about forming a relationship. This was about him getting inside me as soon as possible.

This time, when our gazes clashed, he advanced.

I retreated. Not to get away, but so I backed into the solid wall. I had a good four or five inches on Bookstore Dude—and another forty pounds of pure muscle—but the look on his face warned me he meant business.

He pressed his hands against my chest, anchoring me to the wall. As he raised his chin, I lowered mine.

Our gazes met and held. So many turbulent emotions swirled in those deep-blue irises. I read doubt—and that made me hesitate—but I also read determination.

And that revved my engine more than anything else. I didn't even want to contemplate how long it'd been.

So when he snagged my neck and yanked me toward him, I fell metaphorically into the kiss. Our mouths clashed as we each fought for dominance.

He thrust his tongue into my mouth as he yanked on my hair.

And, as predicted, my cock hardened. In turn, I grabbed his ass and dragged him against me.

The kiss went on and on. Exploring and teasing one moment, fierce and passionate the next. Time spun out as need ratcheted up within me. I'd never wanted anyone more in my life than I wanted this man.

Right here.

Right now.

I pulled back and my head hit the wall. Not hard, thank God. Not that it would've stopped me. Nope, nothing was going to halt this...whatever this way. "I want you to fuck me."

His eyes blazed. "Yes. So much that." He winced. "I don't have a condom."

I yanked my wallet out of my back pocket and held out a condom and lube.

He arched a brow.

"Well, I like to be prepared." I wasn't going to tell him how long it'd been. Both packets were starting to show some wear, and I honestly couldn't remember the last hookup. Hell, in this moment of haze and passion, I couldn't pull forth the memory of the last guy.

He cupped my chin and drew me down for another long, drugging kiss. "Strip."

I quickly surveyed my clothes.

"Just the jeans...it'll be hotter that way."

And awkward, but I was game. Whatever got him inside me the fastest was high on my list. I unzipped my jeans, yanked them and my underwear down to my knees, and palmed my cock.

His eyes grew impossibly wide.

I slid my thumb across my slit, capturing a drop of precum. Deliberately and slowly, I raised it to my mouth and sucked.

He palmed his dick through his khaki pants.

"Make it good." With that, I turned my back to him.

He growled this time.

Such a fucking sexy sound. I placed my hands against the wall and stuck out my ass. My cock ached, and I hoped he wouldn't make me wait long.

Within moments, the whisper of a zipper lowering.

His fingers touching my nape startled me, even though I expected them. He skittered them down my back and lower still. He grabbed my ass and squeezed. Then he leaned against me, and his button-down shirt brushed my skin. "I want to fuck you senseless, but I also need to prep you. I don't know if we have enough lube."

We had plenty of lube, but his words made me wonder if he'd ever hooked up like this, or if his sexual escapades had all been restricted to a bedroom with a bottle of lube at hand.

"Don't prep me, just fuck me." I loved the burn and reveled in the carnality. I needed him to get a move on, and whatever words it took, I'd happily offer them up.

To my shock, he kissed my neck.

"Okay."

The word was an affirmative, but the hesitation was noticeable. I wanted to reassure him. To tell him this was always my preference. That my round of bed partners always knew the score, and that's why I chose them. If this guy offered me tenderness, I wasn't sure what I'd do. Possibly lose my boner.

Possibly enjoy myself.

Possibly develop feelings for him.

Hence the wham, bam, thank you, ma'am. Or sir.

He pulled back, and I heard the tearing of the foil packet.

After a moment, it fell at my feet.

Thank God he understood mess didn't matter. I had plenty of time to clean up before customers arrived.

A second packet tore, and I imagined him slathering lube on his cock. Then, to my surprise, he ran his finger down my crack and slipped it inside.

I adjusted my stance as wide as my clothing would allow.

He slid a second finger inside.

Jesus, it felt good, but I wanted more.

Before the words could leave my mouth, he scissored his fingers.

Okay, the beginning of a burn.

He angled them, twisted them and, fuck me, hit my prostate. Like a pro, he hit it unerringly.

Pleasure sang through my veins and my cock hardened further. I mightn't have thought it possible, but apparently it really liked where we were headed.

I pressed my forehead against the wall. "Please." I wasn't above begging. I needed more, and I needed it now.

He withdrew his fingers, and a deep emptiness welled within me. Knowing he'd fill it again quickly didn't alleviate the feeling of loss. So much loss in my life. If this was the best way for me to connect with people, I had no problems with that. Pathetic? Maybe. But I'd take whatever I could get.

His cockhead nudged my entrance as he slowly pushed in.

Fuck this shit.

I pushed back, attempting to impale myself on him.

The burn I craved lit through me, settling my restless soul. This. This was what I needed.

"Spike, I..."

"Just fuck me." I almost uttered his name. It suited him, but I didn't want to grow intimacy between us. I needed to be taken to oblivion, and he was the guy to do it.

Then, as if a switch flipped in his brain, he did exactly what I needed him to. He grabbed my hips and began thrusting in earnest. Each push forced me against the brick wall. Each slam brought me closer to my orgasm. I wanted to make it good for him as well, but in that moment, I wasn't sure how.

When his hand left my hip, he slid it around my waist, and encircled my cock. Even that simple contact sent my synapses firing.

He squeezed, I panted. He twisted, I bucked.

And still he continued to drill me.

"Dickens, I'm coming." Said through gritted teeth as I struggled to hold back.

"Do it," he growled.

I wasn't known for being an obedient guy, but this time I happily obliged. The orgasm ripped through me, and my cum spurted against the wall.

He continued to nurse me through the climax even as his thrusts increased in franticness. Then, suddenly, he held himself still.

I knew.

His breathing was harsh against my shoulder and then, without warning, his teeth settled on the fleshy part and he applied pressure. Not enough to break skin. Likely not even enough to leave a mark.

But enough that I'd feel it later and know he claimed me.

Without warning, he withdrew.

I winced.

His hand was on my back, but not in a soothing gesture. No, he was telling me not to turn around. He withdrew it, and a moment later, a knotted condom fell at my feet. The sound of a zipper. Then the squeak of his shoes as he left.

The door slammed.

Well, then.

I leaned against the wall. Not just for support, but for the cool against my heated skin. That'd been one of the hottest sexual encounters in my thirty-five years and also, perversely, one of the least satisfying. I wanted... To hold him. For him to hold me. For, God help me, cuddles. Something to assure me we'd resolved our differences. Something that promised we'd do it again.

As I righted myself, I made a vow. We'd do that again. And again and again and again.

Until I got Dickens out of my system once and for all.

Chapter Five

Dickens

Goddamn arrogant asshole.

Referring to yourself or him?

Or both?

Fuck off.

I often held epic discussions with myself in my head, and apparently today was going to be one of *those* days. I pushed through the front door, only belatedly realizing I hadn't locked it when I stormed out to confront Spike. Holy shit. Someone could've come along and taken everything while I was fucking Spike against the wall.

And fucking was the right word. I'd let the animal side of my brain take over. Gave in to the need to dominate. To claim. To own.

Which made no sense. I was angry with the man for playing rock music half the night. That in no way explained why I'd felt the need to be inside him as quickly as I could.

I halted mid-stride.

But it'd felt so good. I couldn't remember the last time I'd been intimate with someone. A hookup during the winter, if I remembered correctly. Some random guy I met on Davie Street in Vancouver when I'd been lonely and headed into the big city to scratch an itch. I'd wound up back at random guy's apartment and we'd had a night of fun. In the morning, when I'd slunk away, I hadn't offered my phone number, and he hadn't asked for it.

Before that? I'd been seeing a guy regularly from Chilliwack. Not exactly long distance, but not convenient either, especially during the rainy season. I wasn't one for adventure. Nope. I was here, and I was content. I needed for nothing. I was comfortable with my life. Did I jerk off a lot? Yes. Did I wish for a warm body? Sure. Was I going to beg motorcycle dude to get sweaty and naked in my sheets?

Fuck, no.

The bells drew my attention. Sunshine stepped into the store with the sun streaming in behind her. The light drew the blueish tinge from her hair. All natural. The woman was stunning. And brilliant. And funny and kind and had a dozen other wonderful attributes.

Colton Pritchard is an asshole.

She removed her sunglasses, gave me the once-over, smiled, and said, "Well, glad to see someone got lucky this morning."

Don't blush. Don't blush. Don't... Too late. Heat raced from my chest up my neck and spread across my cheeks.

She winked. Then meandered over to the window where she cooed and petted my ever-grateful cat.

Ari stretched then head-butted Sun's hand.

I spun around. "Coffee?" I said the word as I headed into the back room.

"Oh, darn."

I turned back to see her escaping out the front door. What now?

I didn't have long to wait as she returned with two Starbucks cups and a little paper bag. She handed me the bag and the cup. "Chocolate croissant, heated up."

These were my favorite, but I was never comfortable with her buying me things. Did I pick up things for her? Sure. But she was my employee. That, and chocolate croissants held a lot of calories.

"To make up for all the energy you expended when you…" She cocked her head and this time the blush crept across her face.

For one horrible moment, I worried she envisioned the whole thing. She wasn't psychic, but she was a sensitive. Her ability to sense emotions, no matter how hidden, was prescient. That and knowing the gender of babies, forecasting good gossip, and predicting who was likely to break up.

Too bad she didn't see her own marriage ending.

But she'd always admitted to having a blind spot for herself and the clearest view of her sisters. The rest of the world fell somewhere in the middle, and that meant she meddled far more than was wise.

Finally, at length, she smiled. A wicked grin. A little more than I was accustomed to. "Well, I told you that you'd be compatible."

With that, she pivoted to flip the open sign and headed into the back room. "I'm jacking up the air conditioning. It's going to be a barn burner, as they say. You should plan to take a few bottles of cold water over to your new boyfriend."

I wasn't sure which part of that sentence annoyed me more—the fact she wanted me to take care of him, or the fact she believed we formed some kind of relationship after one fuck. Still, her comments weren't easily discounted. She claimed she couldn't predict the future, but that wasn't true. I could think of two or three—or more—times in the past ten years when she'd been right on the nose about something. Something unpredictable. Even things that'd been unlikely or, in one case, I would've said impossible. Funny, after all this time, I'd learned to roll with it. To accept she saw the universe in ways I never could.

Would it be great if she could predict sports-team wins or the stock market or the winning lottery ticket numbers? Of course. Would I settle for the heads-up that my parents were planning to retire, and I needed to prepare to take over the business? Yeah, that warning from her came at the perfect time. I'd been contemplating a few things that'd take me away from Mission City. And my parents would've encouraged me. But that would've meant putting off their dreams, and I'm so glad Sun stuck her nose in it. I later discovered my parents had said nothing to her. She'd just known.

Whatever.

A motorcycle engine revved.

Sunshine passed by me and laid a hand on my shoulder.

Yeah, today was going to be a long day.

Yet silence reigned after that, and I settled into my work.

Miss Edna paid us an unexpected visit. The woman was eighty if she was a day.

She'd taught almost fifty years in the Mission City district and, although she retired before I started, I'd heard stories.

She spent most of her time hanging out at the library these days, where the librarians Loriana and Marnie took good care of her.

Few items caught her fancy that she couldn't get from the library, but occasionally I was able to find something that was too obscure for the library to be able to justify acquiring.

They were always on a tight budget.

"Good morning, Miss Edna."

She waved her cane in my direction and headed for one of the comfortable overstuffed chairs.

Immediately, as soon as she settled, Ari leapt onto the arm and demanded scritches.

Miss Edna was always very happy to oblige my nosy cat.

"Could I make you a cup of tea?"

She waved me off, but then held up her hand. "Do you have iced tea?"

"Of course." Powder and not great tasting, but she'd had it before and hadn't complained. In fact, in all the years I'd known her, I couldn't remember her ever saying anything untoward.

I prepared the iced tea, adding plenty of ice, and came back out into the store.

Miss Edna sat with Ari in her lap. The cat purred loudly and the elderly lady had her eyes closed.

I was about to place the glass on a coaster on the side table, when her eyes popped open. She held out a shaky hand, and I gave her the glass. She'd never spilled anything, but I wouldn't care if she did.

She had free rein in this place. Always had and always would.

"What can I help you with today?"

"I'm looking for something special for Marnie."

The younger librarian.

"Well, I'm sure we can help."

"I want the newest R.D. Watts book."

"Okay." I weighed my next words. "I'm quite certain the library bought multiple copies."

She waved her hand. "Of course they did. But I want to get a copy of the limited-edition book. Autographed, of course."

"Of course." Didn't everyone? The books were a hot commodity, and everyone was clamoring for a copy. "I don't see why you think I can help."

"Rainbow went to school with Raven."

Ah, so she thought my employee had the inside track because her sister knew the author. That might be possible, but Sunshine would never try to work that angle.

Raven had a standing invitation to read here whenever she wanted and to do signings whenever it tickled her fancy. She rarely did either.

The first couple of books she published under the penname had gone unnoticed.

Oh, Mission City residents enjoyed the books—they just didn't know the author was in their midst.

An intrepid reporter in town, Sunshine's younger sister Spring, figured it out. She was taking a class at the University of the Fraser Valley where Raven instructed. Spring nabbed an essay written by her prof, picked up her copy of R. D. Watts's book, and fed them into a machine-learning-software program that she begged for time on.

I heard she might've traded favors, although obviously not the sexual kind.

Or I hoped not.

Anyway, the computer confirmed Spring's hypothesis.

She managed to convince the editor of the Mission City Dispatch to run with the story.

They asked for Raven's comment.

When she saw she was about to be outed, she fessed up.

From then on, we couldn't keep the shelves stocked.

Fans flocked from everywhere for a chance to see Raven or get a signed copy.

If I thought she was comfortable, I'd have asked her to sign every copy.

But she was reticent. Partly because she wanted to keep the copies she did sign exclusive, and partly because she couldn't fathom why so many people wanted signed copies. Despite her success, the woman was humble.

Or played herself off as such.

"I didn't realize Marnie was such a fan."

Miss Edna shrugged. "Young lady would never say as much, but I can tell. When she thinks I'm not looking, I'm observing her."

Sounds creepy to me.

Still, a sale was a sale, and anything that made Miss Edna happy earned me brownie points in the cosmic universe. "I'll talk to Sunshine." More likely I'd talk to Raven directly, but I didn't want Miss Edna thinking she could use me as a conduit.

"Talk to Sunshine about what?" The woman herself exited the backroom with a small stack of children's books to restock the shelf.

"About getting Raven to sign her latest book so I can give it to Marnie Jones."

Sunshine beamed. "Well, I'm not close with her, but I'll give it a shot. Marnie's a fan, eh? Cool." She paused. "How's your stomach doing?"

Miss Edna scowled. "It's fine. Impertinent question."

"Make an appointment with Dr. Raymond." Sunshine gave the older woman a sincere smile. "The good doctor hasn't heard from you for a while, so you're due." With that, she swished away on a swirl of her long, flowing, flowery skirt.

The sound Miss Edna made sounded like a combination of a har-rumph and *interfering woman* muttered under her breath.

Yet somehow, deep in my gut, I knew she'd make the phone call. And that it'd be in her best interest to do so. "Were you wanting something for Loriana as well?"

Miss Edna shook her head. "It's Marnie's birthday."

I cocked my head. "How'd you find that out?"

"I have my ways."

The young librarian was one of the most intensely private people I'd ever met, so that piqued my curiosity. "When do you need it by?"

"Next Friday."

Which gave me a week and a half. As long as Raven didn't mind, I'd give it my best shot. I'd drop Miss Edna's name. Maybe even Marnie's. For all her aloofness, Raven liked helping members of the community.

"In the meantime, would you like me to pick something for you? I have several new large-print books, including a romance from a Vancouver Island author."

She eyed me. Then, after what felt like an interminable amount of time, she sighed. "I can't anymore. Even with the special glasses. The glaucoma is too far advanced."

I'd noticed her irises getting cloudy but hadn't commented.

"Would you like me to download an audiobook onto my iPod for you?"

She shook her head and withdrew one from her rather large purse. "Someone donated several to the library, and those nice young girls let me keep this one. On loan."

Probably permanently. If I thought the offer wouldn't be rejected, I'd happily buy her one. "What are you listening to?"

She looked around. "That young Marnie has me hooked on J.D. Robb novels."

I saw nothing scandalous in those. "Oh?"

"They have sex."

Ah. "Well, I'll leave you to it. If you need anything, just wave, and Sunshine or I will be happy to help. Washroom's in the back."

Employee only, but I'd never tell her that. Whatever she needed, we provided.

She inserted her earphones, waved me off, and hit play.

I'd no notion of how long she'd stay, but that was fine. I gave Ari a subtle nod, and the cat blinked back lazily at me. Miss Edna couldn't have a pet at the congregate living facility—which I thought was a travesty—so she'd adopted Ari. She visited often, claiming she worried the cat was lonely.

Yeah, the cat who had humans doing her bidding twenty-four/seven? Unlikely.

As my presence was no longer required, I headed to the computer behind the counter. I did my best to compose an email that didn't sound desperate, but also conveyed the gravity of the request. Hopefully Raven would respond shortly, and I'd know one way or the other.

A motorcycle revved.

Yeah, I was in for another long day.

Chapter Six

Spike

I tried to stay focused.

Truly.

Honestly.

Also impossible.

All day I kept glancing over to the wall. I'd washed off the cum and scrubbed it clean, but I was sure customers could tell. Smell it in the air. See it all over my face. The Cheshire cat grin I couldn't hide. Yeah, forgetting wasn't at all in the realm of possibilities.

My ass was sore.

In all the best ways.

So yeah, forgetting Bookstore Dude and his magical cock wasn't likely to happen. And to think, I hadn't even seen it. Part of me felt that was a deficiency that needed to be rectified. Part of me swore I'd never seen him again.

Yeah, and part of me was laughing at all of it. Of course I'd find a way to see him again. And if groveling was required to have a repeat, I was okay with that. Or I could goad him again. That'd been quite successful.

Kendra was my last customer of the day. The story she gave me was convoluted, but her estranged father was trying to buy his way back into her life after a prolonged absence and had bought her a Kawasaki. She thought it was cute, but wanted to trade it in for a Harley.

Her brother was furious about all of this and wanted her to sell the motorcycle immediately and never ride one again. Since she was twenty-one, she didn't have to listen to Noel. Where did I fit in? She wanted me to spruce up the bike and sell it for her. Taking a commission, of course.

I had no qualms about that. She'd be responsible for coming up with the difference in price or, if she bought an old bike in need of repairs, paying for me to do the work. Any way I looked at it, I did well.

As I met the glare of a furious Noel, I reconsidered how much money I'd be making versus the hassle involved. His coloring was identical to his sister's and Bookstore Dude's. Blond hair, blue eyes. Only he was about six inches shorter than me. About Dickens's height.

Wrong thought.

Kendra was tall. As tall as her brother, only she wore boots with a heel, so she topped him by an inch. That just seemed to piss him off more.

"If you could just sell the Kawasaki, that would be great." Noel's contribution.

"And find me a Harley," Kendra added.

He fixed his glare on his sister. "I told you, that's not happening. Do you understand how dangerous these machines are? Aunt Lucille used to refer to riders as *organ donors*. Do you know what that means?"

Kendra rolled her eyes. "Aunt Lucille is ancient. Things are much safer now."

"Be respectful. She was a trauma nurse for thirty years. She knows of what she speaks."

I rolled my eyes. "Kendra and I signed the paperwork earlier today. Unless you can prove she's not capable of making her own decisions, it's a done deal."

"She has seven days to withdraw from the contract."

"That's right." I scratched my cheek. "*She* has the right. Not you. She's of legal age. Checked her ID." And had run a check to ensure she was the legal owner of the Kawasaki. She was.

"I'm going to make you regret this." Noel's tone was low and menacing.

Kinda hot.

"Do your best." I exuded a confidence I didn't feel. Kendra and Noel were Mission City born and bred. They could both do a lot to damage a newcomer's reputation.

Kendra's blue eyes flashed. "We have a contract. I expect you to email me when you've worked out all the options. I'm buying a Harley."

She glared at her brother, daring him to argue.

He stepped right into her personal space. "Over my dead body."

"Done." Her expression was positively gleeful as she flounced out of my store. Somehow she timed it perfectly, and as the bus pulled up to the stop, she gave a little wave.

The driver was only too happy to have such a lovely woman wearing all leather step into his vehicle.

Well, if the goofy grin on his face was any indication.

"Brat." Half muttered, half cursed.

I held in the laugh. I nearly managed to hold in the smile, but the corners of my mouth twitched.

He glared. Yet something in those blue eyes flared as well. He cocked his head and looked me up and down. Finally, when our gazes clashed again, his eyebrow rose.

Yeah, me too. But you don't do it for me. I only want Bookstore Dude.

As if reading me correctly, he nodded. "I'm happy you're here, because we always need company, but I'm pissed as hell that you're helping my sister. Anything I can do to dissuade you?"

"I was debating putting out a rainbow flag. Too obvious?"

Another cock of the head. "Mission City is moving towards progressive, but you're still in the Bible Belt of the Fraser Valley. Some are welcoming, some tolerate, some are hostile." He glanced around the shop. "No idea how your clientele would feel. You out?"

A rather personal question. But one I didn't mind answering. "I'm not in. I just don't advertise." I scratched my nose. "You?"

"Yeah. I run a marketing firm and work for several local businesses. Some chose me because they want to be seen as more inclusive. I don't mind being the poster boy if it makes Mission City more welcoming." He eyed me again. "We don't have a club or anything, but a few of us keep in touch. You looking? I might be able to introduce—"

I cleared my throat. Better to disabuse him of the notion straight away. "I'm, uh, not as I seem."

This time his entire brow rose. "I wasn't judging."

"And I might've met someone."

Are you nuts? Bookstore Dude is a dud. You'll never make a relationship work with him.

Maybe not. But I was sure going to make an effort.

My gaze must've strayed as we spoke because he looked right at the shared wall. He considered, then he smiled. "I've been hoping Dickens might meet someone."

"Oh, we're not—"

He held up his hand. "I'd never say anything." He ran a hand through his hair.

Much as Dickens had earlier.

"I hope it works out, because you both deserve happiness. Do I wish you weren't enabling my sister? Sure. Can I stop the two of you? Obviously not." He gave one last look around my store and exited. I watched him check the road. When it was clear, he strode across to his nice shiny SUV. Within moments, he pulled out and disappeared.

Well, that was interesting.

I wasn't sure which piqued my interest more—his offer to set me up, or my swift refusal because I felt like I already had someone in my life. I'd keep Noel's offer in my back pocket. If Bookstore Dude turned out to be an epic failure, I could always call Uptight Dude for... What? He offered to hook me up. No, introduce me. I warned him I wasn't what most people expected. Did he understand that meant I liked being dominated? Liked taking it up the ass?

Who cares?

True. If Uptight Dude could set me up, who was I to turn down the offer? Even better if I could find someone I was compatible with.

You're compatible with Dickens.

True. Convincing him of that was a whole new ballgame.

The wall clock showed it was noon. I could afford to close up shop for a half hour. I'd see if Dickens wanted to let me buy him lunch. Maybe we could eat it together.

Yeah, right. Dream on.

Well, I had to try something. Sitting here stewing wasn't going to get me very far. I stalked to the sink and scrubbed my hands until they were almost raw. Took a few minutes, but eventually I was able to scour off most of the grease. I was pretty sure Dickens rarely lifted the hood of his pretty Prius. Probably had a mechanic on standby for all the grubby work.

I removed the leather thong holding my hair and put it on the edge of the sink. Then I combed my hair until it looked decent. I didn't have Noel's preppy look, but I cleaned up decently. *Hopefully he'll notice the effort.* Locking the front door behind me after having secured the gate, I headed next door. The sunlight glared on the front window so I couldn't see inside.

Just do it already.

I cleared my throat and opened the door with as much confidence as I could put into the action, given I felt absolutely none internally.

The door gave way and a light tinkle of bells rang out.

I cringed.

On the right was an arrangement of overstuffed chairs, one of them holding an older woman with gray hair. She glanced my way with kind eyes. She held up her finger, and I waited.

After a moment, she removed one earphone and beckoned me closer.

Hmm. I advanced, bent over...and jumped.

A cat had poked its head up from the woman's lap. It regarded me for a moment, clearly decided I was no threat to the old lady or himself...herself...and resumed its nap.

"I'm Miss Edna. You can call me Miss Edna."

"Yes, ma'am."

She glared.

"Sorry, yes, Miss Edna."

"Now, I'm happy to see you've come calling."

How did she know? Was I wearing a sign? I'd debated bringing flowers but figured Dickens wouldn't be impressed. Was I wrong about that? Before I could respond, she continued.

"Now, she's a fragile one these days. Comes across as fine, but I know he broke her heart."

At my questioning glance, she clarified, "Her ex-husband. He's a good man, but he's too broody for her. She needs someone upbeat and fun." She gave me the once-over. "Can you be fun?"

"Well, I can be funny." Whether by telling witty jokes or self-deprecating humor was a toss up. I offered a smile. "But, Miss Edna, Sunshine isn't my type. At least I assume you're talking about Sunshine."

Her elegantly plucked eyebrow quirked.

Wait for it...

She grinned. Actually grinned.

Almost disconcerting after the dour expression when discussing Sunshine's ex-husband.

"Well, I'll be damned."

I didn't know her well enough to know if a swear word was out of character for her or just her everyday speak. "I hope not, Miss Edna. I'd like to see you ascend when you die."

Her look of dubiousness told stories. Either she didn't believe, or she believed she was already damned and it was therefore too late. Toss up at this point.

"Miss Edna, I'm glad to see you've met our newest resident in town."

Sunshine appeared behind me, and I noted the door she'd obviously just come through. Interesting she left her elderly customer to mind the store.

"He's calling on Dickens."

I sensed no censure from Miss Edna. Only mild curiosity. I glanced at her. Okay, major curiosity.

"Well, Dickens is meeting with Raven right now to get those books signed. Major miracle he was able to get it done for you."

Miss Edna waved her imperious hand in the air. "I knew he could. Or you could."

"All on him." Sunshine bestowed a warm smile upon me. "You're welcome to wait. He just ran over to Abbotsford. Should be back in twenty minutes."

I managed a smile. "No, thank you. I need to be getting back."

Her gaze intensified.

Those pale-blue orbs saw right through me. So transparent. Them and me.

She shrugged. "I'll let him know you were here."

"I'd prefer if you didn't. Seems silly, you know?"

"Young man, anyone who comes calling deserves to be heard. If Sunshine doesn't tell him, I will."

Ah, well, at least I'd been warned. "I'm going to Tim Horton's. Would either of you like something?"

Both women shook their heads.

I bobbed my own and left as quickly as I could.

Your goose is cooked.

Maybe not.

What did you expect?

That he'd be there.

And now?

Time to grab a sandwich and head back to see if I could find an acceptable Harley for Kendra.

Chapter Seven

Dickens

"Another happy customer." Sunshine flounced back into the office. Going way above and beyond, she'd driven Miss Edna over to the library. Far too hot for the elderly lady to walk. Apparently Sun also offered to stay until Miss Edna had given the books to Marnie, but the woman claimed she had a ride home planned with the shuttle bus.

I was cooler, but not by much. Hoofing around campus to secure a limited-edition copy of the book, and Raven's autograph, had taken much out of me.

This weather was nuts for June, and apparently tomorrow was going to be worse. We were promised a thunder shower, but those things rarely materialized. We'd be lucky if we got a few drops.

Which reminded me...

"Sun, are you up to watering the flower bed?"

The city installed one a few years back, but The Owl's Nest took responsibility for it. We had flowers, but we also grew a few herbs. A nice touch.

"Sure, boss." The woman looked as cool as the proverbial cucumber. Maybe the flowy dress? She had bohemian chic down pat.

Today, I didn't stand a chance in my khakis and golf shirt. I needed to give up all semblance of propriety and throw on my shorts and white T-shirt. But I wouldn't. I was raised to believe image in the store meant everything. My father'd worn a tie and my mother a proper dress. The move to khakis was a departure.

Except Sunshine, of course. She'd worn flowy dresses as well as jeans and blouses for as long as she worked here.

My parents never applied the same standards to her.

I glanced down at my disheveled outfit. Might I consider going more casual?

The clientele had changed over the years. We saw many younger people who didn't want to read books on their phones, while their parents embraced technology. The anonymity of an electronic device. And some of our long-time clients, like Miss Edna, were fading away.

I wiped my brow and headed over to the a/c to lower the temperature. The sale of Raven's book would cover the cost. I'd wanted to sell the book at cost to Miss Edna, but she insisted on paying full retail. She gave me *that* glare, and I didn't argue.

As I grabbed my ice-cold water in my stainless-steel water bottle, I remembered Sunshine's warning words from earlier. That I should have plenty of water on hand to give to Spike. Like the older man was my responsibility or something.

Not that much older.

And so your type.

Did I really need the voice in my head admonishing me?

Shut up.

Sun re-entered the store. "You should totally take him a bottle." With that little bombshell, she took the watering can through to the back room.

Damn interfering woman.

And if she said it, then it needed to be acted upon. Likely in the moment.

I followed her into the back room to grab a bottle of water as she headed back into the store.

I discreetly sniffed my pits, which weren't too bad, and braced myself for the onslaught of heat. I strode through the store, purposely ignoring Sun, and headed into the soupy day.

A haze hung over us, here in the lower Fraser Valley.

My parents' home had been up in the mountains north of town, and I would've preferred to live there, but I didn't have the funds, so I got to live down here with the pollution. One day, I promised myself. One day I would live up in the clean air.

My strides were a little less strident as I made my way to Spike's shop. I hoped to find him inside sipping an iced coffee, but no such luck. I followed the sound of cursing, through the open garage door and into the enclosed workspace, open to all the elements. How did he plan to work here in the winter? Actually, likely very few bikes needing repair when it snowed, or the temps hit well below freezing. Maybe he went to Arizona for the winter?

The object of my obsession dropped a wrench on the ground and let out another string of expletives.

"You'll frighten away the customers with that mouth." I reconsidered. "Okay, maybe just some of them."

"Fucking hell." He let out one long breath, then rose and, after a fashion, turned to face me. Despite not being in direct sunlight, his skin was an abnormal lobster-red and his breaths labored.

I made a grab for his arm.

He swayed dangerously.

I advanced again, this time not taking *no* for an answer. I snagged his elbow and, after a moment, he let me lead him inside.

Since the door was open, the inside wasn't much better.

I noted the door to the office, and saying a prayer he had sense, herded him that way.

A blast of cold air hit us as we entered the room. I all but shoved him into the chair, then pivoted to close the door as quickly as possible. I uncapped the bottle and shoved it at him.

Plenty of shoving going on right now and none of it sexual.

Did you really have to go there?

Yep, I did. Aside from the red color of his skin, he was still damn sexy. I didn't mind a bit of sweat. Especially after sexual exertions.

"Not thirsty." He mumbled the words and tried to bat away the water.

A bit spilled onto his shirt.

I growled.

Spike cracked an eye. He took the water bottle. Or tried to.

Guiding the bottle, I held on as Spike drank. Greedily.

"Hey, slow down." I pulled the water back.

This time, Spike growled.

"Relax. Slow sips." I placed the back of my hand on the man's forehead. Way too hot. "We need to get you into a cold shower."

"Will you fuck me in the shower? I have this fantasy..." His words trailed off as his eyes slid shut.

Should I call an ambulance? Or drive him to the hospital?

Calm down.

I knew enough about first aid to get us through this situation. Didn't I? I yanked out my phone and texted Sunshine, asking for help.

Thirty seconds later, the front door to the shop opened.

God, I truly loved the woman.

She stepped into the back room. "He doesn't look so good."

"Do you think he needs to go to the hospital?"

"Am fine. No hospitals." Spike's voice was stronger.

"I'd say start by cooling him down."

"That's the plan." I glanced around the room. "Can you put a sign on the door and lock up? I think if you leave through the back door, you won't need keys."

She gave a brief salute. "All taken care of, boss. Get your man upstairs." She eyed Spike again. "And if he doesn't improve, then yeah, call to get advice. Like if he gets confused, loses consciousness, or can't drink water. Who's your doctor?"

"Owen McCauley." I answered her question.

"You're golden." She made a shooing motion.

I needed no further encouragement. Between the two of us, we managed to get Spike on his feet. I led him around to the stairs up to his apartment. We made it up without too much trouble, and I was fishing in his pocket for his keys when he opened the door.

"You didn't lock your door?"

"Wanted to be able to drag you up for a quickie."

I looked at him incredulously.

"Gotcha." The corners of his mouth turned upward. "I was in a hurry this morning, and wasn't planning to leave the property. I figured I'd hear anyone moving around up here."

"With the racket of your shop and the bikes? Not likely."

"Motorcycles." He corrected me. "And I have to find a Kendra for Harley." He scrunched his forehead. "No, a Harley for Kendra. Not for Noel, though. Uptight prick believes motorcycles are dangerous."

"They are." I'd gone to school with Noel and had no clue Kendra was into motorcycles. But she was much younger than me. "Look, this is a pleasant conversation, but we need to get you stripped and into the shower. Or maybe a bath." I really needed to google heat exhaustion. I didn't even know what his core temperature was.

Interestingly, Spike's apartment was the mirror opposite of mine, and his bathroom was on the outside wall of the building. Always too cold during the deepest winter months.

Where Spike's differed from mine were the luxurious appointments. He had a separate shower and tub, two sinks, and a nice, pretty toilet. And, to top things off, a lovely, frosted glass window.

When I indicated the toilet seat, he sat acquiescently. I turned on the water, carefully gauging temperature. I wanted to cool him down, but I didn't want to shock him with cold. We weren't at that stage.

At least I hoped not.

A hand touching my back startled me. Still crouching, I pivoted back.

"I'm really okay." He rubbed his forehead. "Truly."

"Well, that's great. We'll get you cooled down, and then I'll decide if you're really okay." I snagged the hem of his T-shirt and, with a little help from him, managed to get it over his head.

My breath caught.

Yeah, I'd suspected he was good-looking. Okay, I suspected he was gorgeous.

My imagination hadn't done him justice. Apparently working in a repair shop and riding a motorcycle left a guy ripped. Or he worked out on top of everything else. Man, the guy was perfection.

I, on the other hand, was softer. I walked, listening to audiobooks, but I didn't spend any time at the gym. He hadn't seen me earlier when we'd been fucking, so he didn't know. Maybe he wouldn't find me attractive. Maybe all he cared about was my cock.

Get your head in the game.

The tub was just about full, so I shut off the water. When I reached for the button on his jeans, though, he stilled my hands. "I can do this."

"I'm sure you can, but you're going to let me help."

"Dickens, I—"

I glared.

He relented.

After unbuttoning his jeans, I coaxed him into standing. I unzipped his jeans and dragged them, along with his underwear, down his legs and to the ground. Of his own volition, he stepped out of them and over to the tub. Within moments, he was lowering himself into the chilled water.

He hissed.

"Suck it up. It's the quickest way to cool you down."

Once I was sure he'd stay and also wouldn't pass out and drown, I left him to it. Had I noted the pretty cock nestled in the thatch of dark curls? Absolutely. I wasn't blind. Did I shove that thought aside as I called Dr. MacCauley? Yes to that as well.

"He's on his lunch break," his very officious receptionist informed me after I introduced myself.

"It's kind of urgent."

She chuffed. "Well then, you should go to the urgent care clinic or the hospital. Or you could call the nurse's hotline."

All reasonable suggestions. But I wanted to speak to someone I knew. "Please." I wasn't above begging.

Another chuff. Finally, at length, "Hold, please."

Tinny muzak came through the speaker, and I made a note to tell the doctor that he really needed better hold music. Another day, though.

"Hey Dickens, what's up?"

The relief was instantaneous. "Hey, uh, sorry to bother you."

"No bother. What's happened?"

"Well, I have this...friend...and I think he's suffering from heat exhaustion. Or I don't know, maybe heat stroke...?"

"That can be very serious. Do you know what his core body temperature is?"

I wracked my brain to think if either Spike, from what I'd seen, or I, from what I remembered, had a thermometer. "I don't know. And I don't have a thermometer either."

"Well, you'd have to take the temperature rectally to get an accurate reading."

"What?" God, let me have heard wrong. "I'm pretty sure he'd tell me to fuck off."

"So he's talking? Communicating? Coherently?"

To my knowledge, Spike'd never been a chatty guy, but he seemed okay to me. "Yeah, when he talks, I mostly understand what he's saying."

"Not much of a talker?"

"No, frankly, not."

"Where is he now?"

"In a tepid bath."

"And he seems to be cooling?"

I poked my head inside the bathroom. Spike lay in the bathtub with a towel under his neck. Most of the red color was gone. I quietly slipped back out. "Yeah, I'd say he is."

"Okay. Of course I'd say bring him in, but something tells me if that'd been a possibility, you'd have already done it."

"You know me well, Doc."

He chuckled. "So, monitor him. Any signs of disorientation, call an ambulance. If he can't take in water, or doesn't cool down, don't hesitate. If you're still worried in a couple of hours, I can drop by on my way home."

"I'll keep that in mind."

"Do. And I think you're due to come in soon. It's been a while."

"Haven't done anything worth mentioning." Except I had. Just this morning, in fact. But I'd used a condom, so it didn't count.

Right?

Likely wrong on that belief. It probably did count.

"I'll keep that in mind. Oh—" How to put this tactfully? "—your hold music is appalling."

Owen chuckled. "I think you're feeling calmer. Get some more liquids into your friend, call if you want a visit. I've got to go. One of my regulars just arrived, and I don't like making her wait."

"Yeah, thanks."

What that, he was gone.

And I felt truly alone.

I snagged the abandoned water bottle, added more cold water from the tap, and headed back into the bathroom. Spike was rising from the bathtub, and droplets of water covered his fantastic skin. His arms and neck were a shade darker than his pale skin where the sun didn't touch. Clearly he didn't sunbathe naked. I put the bottle of water on the counter and reached for a towel.

Once he was safely on a bathmat, he took it with some gratitude. Grudging, but there.

"Drink some more water. Do you want clean clothes?" I indicated to the apartment behind me.

"I can get them." He squinted. "But thank you. For all of it."

I backed out of the bathroom and headed toward the kitchen. When at a loss for things to do? Cook.

Chapter Eight

Spike

Stupid, stupid, stupid.
Mom said don't call yourself stupid.
Mom's not here.

No, she wasn't. And that hurt more than anything. Sometimes I missed her a bit, and sometimes that absence was a gaping hole that no companionship could fill. She constantly nagged me when I was a kid to wear sunscreen. She was ahead of her time amongst her sun-worshipping compatriots. And yet she'd been the one to die. She hadn't smoked either. Nor drank to excess. Was just one of those things, the doctors said. I worried back then that my father might die, but no way. He drank, smoked, and lived hard. Especially after Mom died. Didn't they say the good died young? Never more true than for Mareike Marlowe.

I drank the water Bookstore Dude gave me. Dickens. The guy's name was Dickens. I owed him that much—to remember and use his name. I owed him a whole lot more...and that rankled. A lot.

Sorting through my clothes, I selected a T-shirt and sweatpants. Despite my earlier high temperature, I was cooling down. Almost chilled. As I stood in my bedroom, I contemplated just crawling into bed and staying there forever. I would, except I'd left everything unlocked downstairs, and anyone could come in and steal the bikes. I slid the clothes on and eyed my feet. Fuck it. Putting on socks was too much work. I snagged the empty water bottle and headed into the kitchen to refill it and drink more.

I came up short.

Dickens sat on my sofa reading one of my books.

From this distance, I couldn't tell which one, since it was a tome from my Harvard Classics series. Nice to look at, impossible to read. A rash eBay purchase one day when I'd been feeling low and missing Mom. I should've resold the set but never could quite bring myself to part with them.

Dickens laid the book aside and rose gracefully.

He advanced toward me, and I held my ground.

When he was directly in front of me—in my personal space—he reached up to place the back of his hand on my forehead.

I bristled.

But I also let him do it.

"Just hold still," he ordered.

I growled.

"Well, Dr. MacCauley said he would come here and stick a thermometer up your ass if I was worried you weren't cooling down. Or we could go to the hospital."

Shock was the most prominent emotion that ricocheted through me. "I'll, uh, pass on the thermometer. There's only one thing I want in my ass." I gave him a lascivious once-over.

He cocked an eyebrow, and he also removed his hand. "You seem cooler."

Before I could respond, he grabbed the water bottle and headed to the faucet.

"I can do that." My protest sounded weak, even to my ears. I liked he was taking care of me. Mom died when I was nine, and I didn't remember anyone else ever taking care of me.

"I'm quite sure you can, but you should sit down."

"I'd rather lie down."

"Well, that'll work as well. On the couch or on the bed? You need rest."

Truthfully, I felt okay. Probably better than I deserved. I still couldn't believe I'd been that stupid. But I wanted the Kawasaki tuned perfectly before the potential buyer came to see it tomorrow. And I'd gotten to cleaning it and...time got away from me. "Look, I'm really sorry."

He turned back, handed me the water bottle, and indicated the bedroom.

"I, uh, have to...you know..."

He snagged the bottle and pointed to the bathroom.

Phew.

I could say the word piss, of course. Except he just seemed a little too prim and proper for that, and I owed him respect. He was here, I was grateful, and I needed to do everything in my power to show that gratitude.

When I was finished in the bathroom, I wandered into the bedroom.

He sat in the chair by the window while the water bottle sat on the nightstand. He looked up from his book and inclined his head. "Please drink some more. If you're able to keep that down and you stay lucid, I'll call Dr. MacCauley and let him know you're okay."

I sat on the bed with my back against the headboard and my legs stretched out before me. "That's very nice of you. Of him. I mean, I don't even know him. He doesn't know me."

You don't know me.

Except in the biblical sense.

"Owen's a good man. Newer in town. I saw him for a bout of pneumonia when Dr. Raymond was out of town, and I liked him. I asked if I could see him in the future and he said sure. Dr. Raymond is always fully booked, so he had no problem with it." Dickens rose and moved to my side of the bed. He pressed his hand again to my forehead. A sigh escaped his lips. "Much better." His eyes turned to blue flint. "You scared the shit out of me."

"I'm sorry." I rubbed my forehead. "Really sorry." Contrition hurt, but I owed him this much.

"I don't need your apology. Just a promise to never do that again. You scared Sunshine." He ducked his head. "And me."

"Please tell Sunshine that I apologize as well."

"Oh, I'm sure you'll have the opportunity. She's likely to *drop by* tomorrow to see how you're doing."

I smacked my forehead, then tried to rise.

A finger to my chest pushed me back down. I was weaker than I realized. "But I need to lock up. Otherwise everything'll be gone."

He offered a slight smile. "Uh, Sunshine locked up." He pulled my set of keys from his pocket and dropped them onto the nightstand. "She even put a sign in the window explaining your absence and telling potential customers to drop into The Owl's Nest for more information. If there are people looking, she'll encourage them to come back later. She's a great salesperson."

"She's a great person."

"That she is. I'm lucky to have her."

"Any chance I can poach her?"

He tilted his head in question.

"I need help. The books—" I gestured wildly toward the living room. "—are a mess."

He scratched his nose. "I know someone who might be able to help. She used to work for my parents, but quit to have her kids. Her youngest just started kindergarten. I suspect she'd like something to occupy her time."

Could it be that simple? "You'll put in a good word?"

"I'll ask Darlene personally. She's a whiz with numbers, and we were sorry to lose her. I was considering trying to lure her back." He glanced around before meeting my gaze again. "But you seem to need her more."

Ah, so he'd spotted the pile of papers on the kitchen table. I'd taken to eating in front of the television on the couch so I didn't have to look at the disaster.

I took a long pull of water before settling. "Would you...?" Jesus, was I really going to ask him this? "Would you read to me?"

His eyes softened. "Sure, I can do that." He snagged the crocheted blanket from the end of my bed and laid it over me, taking special care to cover my feet. "You'll cool down as you rest. If you're too hot, we can take the blanket off."

Truth was, I was chilled. Having the blanket my grandmother made for me also brought comfort. I was raw right now. Vulnerable. This gave me a modicum of protection.

Unexpectedly, he feathered his hand through my hair, then lazily dragged his knuckles down my cheek.

I couldn't remember ever feeling so cherished—so special. Our gazes held for another moment before he moved over to the chair.

He was about to retake his seat when I spoke.

"Join me?"

He cocked an eyebrow.

My cheeks flamed. "No, not for that."

He didn't succeed in suppressing his grin of mischievousness. "Well, sure, I can join you." He sat on the bed.

At some point, he'd removed his shoes.

I like that he'd made himself at home. Somehow that made this strange afternoon more normal.

He picked up the book and squinted.

"You need reading glasses?"

I was treated to an eye roll.

"My vision is terrible. I have progressives, but sometimes I have to get the angle right." He adjusted and, after a moment, settled into a more relaxed stance. He held up the book. "I hope you don't mind poetry. I can grab one of the others—"

I placed a restraining hand on his arm. "This is perfect."

Our gazes held yet again and, after a moment, he nodded. He cleared his throat and began to read.

John Keats.

Mom's favorite. My first memories were of her reading to me. Simple picture books at first. Then on to chapter books. Eventually she moved to poetry and novels. Yes, I'd only been a child, but she instinctively understood I craved words. Words I could only learn by her saying them to me.

As Dickens's gentle voice washed over me, I let the memories of her wash over me. I spent so much time pushing her from my consciousness, but just this once I let her be center stage. My longing was acute. Like I'd lost her yesterday and not seventeen long years ago. I'd had much more time without her than with her, yet she always played a critical part in my life. I liked to believe she'd have supported me coming out. She would've cheered when I got my motorcycle-repair license. She would've been the first in line to see me opening this store.

A tear slipped out and tracked down my cheek. I didn't move to wipe it away, lest I draw attention to myself. I wanted him to keep reading. Forever. Soon his words became harder to understand, and soon after that, I was pulled under.

When I awoke, I found myself alone.

Like always.

The book lay on the bed next to me, and I idly picked it up. In the diffuse light of the late afternoon sun through my blinds, I struggled to make sense of the words. I wanted Dickens back. Regret slammed into me that he'd been reading and I missed much of it. Or maybe he stopped as soon as I fell asleep. I checked the bedside clock. Almost six o'clock. I'd been down for the better part of the afternoon. I'd never sleep tonight.

My bladder made itself known, and I slipped into the bathroom. After pissing, I washed my hands and inspected myself in the mirror. I didn't shave, but I kept my beard short. I scratched my cheeks. Time for a trim.

This weekend.

God, we weren't even halfway through the week. Initially I planned to be open seven days a week, but that was crazy. I might not have a social life, but I needed downtime. Weekends were busy in Mission City, so I figured I'd close Mondays. If I was able to hire this Darlene woman, she could work that day, and if I was needed, she could call me if an emergency repair came in.

I ran my hand through my overlong hair, pulled it into a thong, and headed into the living room.

And, for the second time today, came up short.

Dickens was unpacking the most-heavenly smelling food and sorting it onto plates. Something alerted him to my presence, and he looked up. "Oh, good. I didn't want to wake you, but I would have. You'll never sleep tonight. I got Chinese from the place across the way."

I'd eyed the restaurant several times but figured buying for one was a waste. But sharing for two? Much more logical.

"I should pay." Only fair, given he'd forgone a day of work to take care of my sorry ass.

"You can get it the next time."

Said so casually. As if assuming there'd be another time. That we'd repeat the ritual of eating together on a regular basis.

Did I want that?

Hell, fucking, yes.

"Sure." I stood awkwardly with my hands resting against the back of a kitchen chair. The table had been cleared, and a nice stack of organized papers sat on the desk.

Dickens followed my gaze. "I might've done some preliminary sorting. And Darlene will be here for an interview in the morning. She can start a couple of days a week until your business picks up, and then she'll be happy for the work." A dark expression passed over his normally sunny face. "She's going through a rough patch. Now, don't tell her I said that, and please don't hire her out of pity. She's a hard worker, and you'll get your money's worth. She'll have you whipped into shape in no time."

I believed him.

He placed two plates, heaped high with food, on the table. "I checked your kitchen, and although there wasn't much, I also figured you didn't have any problems eating meat or anything like that. Allergies?"

"What...uh, no." He'd gone through my kitchen? Had worried about my food preferences? Who was this guy, and what had he done with angry Bookstore Dude? I sat and eyed the plate. "I think you even picked my favorites." I inhaled deeply. "Yep, I think you've pretty much nailed me."

"Well, not in the past day or so..." He let his words hang as he settled in the seat next to me. He gave me a wicked wink and then dug into a mouthful of sweet and sour pork.

"Are you saying I might get a repeat?" I perked up.

"Let's see how you're doing later. You went through a big ordeal today, and your body's still recovering."

"No." I shook my head. "My body's doing just fine. Better than fine. All ready to go."

He deliberately eased away and leaned over to scrutinize my growing erection. He snickered as he sat back. "Horny much?"

"Around you? Pretty much all the time."

His jaw slackened.

Too blunt? "Look, I'm not someone who goes around thinking about sex all the time. Like, I've been so busy the last little while—"

"How long?"

"How long?"

"Since you've had sex?" He scratched his nose. "With someone other than me."

Damn. Stole my pithy response. I squinted my left eye. "I plead the fifth?"

He snickered. "You're not an American, and I doubt your answer will self-incriminate. Unless you did something nefarious."

It took a moment for me to realize he was serious. "No, nothing. I'm pretty boring. Well, I like it rough and I like to receive, but other than that, pretty boring. You?" I doubted Mr. Uptight'd done anything *nefarious* but better I find out his predilections now.

"Boring. But I suspect you knew that. The occasional tryst, but nothing for a while. And no one serious since university."

And I could spot a story, but I didn't want to pry.

"Why did Keats make you cry?"

His question was so out of left field that I gaped. Talk about personal. And yet, in that moment, being honest felt right.

"I have dyslexia. A severe case. I can hardly read."

His expression turned compassionate.

I didn't want his sympathy, and wished I could take the words back.

"Darlene will get your paperwork organized." He looked around. "You've done okay for yourself."

"My old boss Gia read all the contracts and did much of the negotiating. She said I could keep asking her for help, but I want to stand on my own, you know?"

"I do know." He slipped his hand over my clenched fist. "I'll be here to help. Hell, Sunshine might be flighty, but she's got a great nose for business. You don't have to be alone again."

"You make it sound so simple."

"Because it is." He squeezed my hand, let it go, then resumed eating as if he hadn't just blown my world apart.

Chapter Nine

Dickens

Should I have asked him about the tears?

Possibly not.

Probably not.

And yet I couldn't regret the question. I passed off the dyslexia like it was no big deal because I suspected he didn't want me to comment. So I accepted it as fact, pointed out Darlene would be perfect, and moved on.

Should I have told him he never had to be alone again?

Possibly not.

Probably not.

And yet I couldn't regret my statement. I didn't want to leave him alone. I wanted to spend more time with him. Get to know him. Find out what made him tick. What made him laugh. What else made him cry. Ridiculous as it sounded, I was looking into the future and seeing him as part of it. And that didn't scare me. I hadn't had a man seriously in my life since Isaac. Now, within days of meeting this annoying man, I wanted something permanent with him.

Well, annoying was too strong a word. Irritating? Even that felt too harsh. He just had quirks—like playing music too loud—but that was something we could compromise on.

Right?

You're getting way ahead of yourself.

True. Hell, I didn't even know if I was welcome here or making a pest of myself.

We continued to eat in silence. My call had thrilled Darlene.

Apparently her husband had just lost another job, and things were tight. He wouldn't be happy about her working, but they needed the money.

I had strong opinions about the man, but I always kept my own counsel. If she ever saw the truth and left, Sunshine and I would be there to support her. I suspected Spike would be in that camp as well.

"What's your name?"

His fork clattered to the plate.

I grinned. "A mother who read you Keats did *not* name you Spike."

A shadow crossed his expression.

I instantly regretted my words said in jest.

He swept his arm in the air as if shooing away a fly. "She passed a long time ago."

"I'm sorry." God, such a trite thing to say.

His sad, dark-brown eyes met mine. "Yeah, me too. I wish it'd been my dad and not her, but we don't get to make choices like that."

"But you've chosen to honor her." I might've been extrapolating a lot, but the love was so clear to see.

"If I honored her, I'd use the name she gave me."

"Which was...?" He was killing me.

"Fritz."

I nearly burst out laughing. I held it in, though, but it was a near thing.

His expression told me that I wasn't fooling anyone.

"She loved Swiss Family Robinson." He pushed some rice around on his plate. "I watch the film now, and I see how the natives were treated, and I think about colonialism." He cleared his throat. "But as a kid, I remember watching the movie with Mom and loving it. I thought it was cool to be named after a character in a book. Until I got to school and all the kids made fun of me. Mom tried to soothe the hurt, but between that and the fact I couldn't read...well, school was hell for me. After mom died, I quit trying. I did the minimum it took to pass each grade, and the day I graduated I came out to my dad. As I expected, he booted me out. At least he gave me a couple hundred and enough time to pack a suitcase. I came down here and made a life for myself."

So much to unpack. Was now the time? I should've been more prudent in asking him his name. Still, how was I supposed to know what a can of worms I might open?

He waved again. "No big deal, okay?" He met my gaze directly. "I don't regret anything in my life because it brought me to this point, and I'm fucking happy here."

I spotted no prevarication. No wavering. Nothing to indicate he was anything but sincere. I'd have to take him at his word.

"Did you order dessert?"

Having just consumed a massive amount of food, I didn't have room for dessert. And I hadn't thought to order anything. "Uh, no."

He clapped his hands together. "Great. I clean up, you...do whatever you need to do...and we meet in my bedroom in five minutes." His grin slipped. "Oh, what about your cat?"

"Sunshine took Aristotle home tonight. Just in case you needed me to stay with you."

"I love your diligent employee, and I definitely need you to stay with me tonight." His grin was wicked.

Well, that was blunt. But I loved that about him. He said what was on his mind. I needed to do that more often.

Love? Strong word. I loved he was blunt, but did I love him? Had enough time passed for that? Maybe not. Whatever this was, though, I wanted more.

I rose, nodded, and wordlessly headed to the bathroom. I'd showered this morning and, despite all the stress, hadn't sweated much today. I pissed, washed my hands, then grabbed the toothpaste and put a bit on my finger. Okay, so this was so tacky, but I wanted our second kiss to be nice. I didn't want to worry about bad breath.

Were we even going to kiss? We'd fucked. Hard. And we'd had a clashing of the mouths, but that hadn't really been a kiss. Nothing like leisurely exploration. Nothing like a *getting to know you* kiss. What if he just wanted me to pound into him again? I mean, he seemed up to the exertions. He certainly appeared to carry no lingering effects from his earlier episode. Was I overthinking this? I had a tendency to do that.

Once my teeth were clean, I washed my hands again, sniffed my pits, straightened my shirt, and headed into Spike's bedroom.

Fritz's bedroom.

Surprisingly, the name fit him. Yes, he wasn't a blue-eyed blond. He was dark and broody. Yet, Fritz was far more suitable than Spike.

Whatever his name was, he lay on his bed. He'd pulled the comforter back, and he lay on the top sheet. Buck naked. Stroking his erect cock. "How do you want me?"

Any way I can get you.

A worthy sentiment, but unnecessary to speak aloud. Actions spoke louder than words anyway, right? So as I unbuttoned my shirt, I held his gaze—telegraphing my intention.

He spread his legs open and flexed his hips. Oh yeah, he understood.

I laid the shirt on the chair I'd sat in earlier. Then I unbuckled my belt. I lowered my zipper and removed my pants and underwear in one quick motion.

Still, I held his gaze.

I balanced myself on the back of the chair while removing my socks.

"Feet are so fucking sexy."

Uh...so not going to go there. If he found my feet sexy, I guess that was all right.

He dragged his thumb across his slit, collected precum, and slid the digit into his mouth.

That was sexy as fuck. I palmed my cock in anticipation.

He pointed to the condoms and lube on the nightstand. "Did a run to the drugstore yesterday after work."

In other words, after we'd fucked. Good, he didn't have a stash on hand. I wasn't the jealous type, but I also didn't want to think about him with anyone else. Nope. He was all mine. And I intended to see it remained that way.

I crawled up the bed until I hovered over him.

"I'm fine, Dickens, honestly." He grinned ruefully. "I swear that's never happened before, and it'll never happen again."

"See that it doesn't." Of course I intended to keep a close eye on him. I didn't need another fright like that.

He pressed his thumb to my brow. "Will you fuck me already?"

Just to be certain, I placed my hand against his forehead. Cool to the touch.

He snickered. "You're about to make me hot and bothered, so don't be thinking of checking later."

"There are other ways to check."

He cringed, and I winced. Yeah, so totally inappropriate.

Then he arched his hips up to meet mine, and our cocks brushed. *Heaven.*

I lowered myself over him, and he opened his legs farther to welcome me. Like coming home. Somewhere comfortable. Somewhere familiar. Somewhere I wanted to return to again and again. As I dove in for a kiss, he snickered.

Surprised, I stopped.

"Just thinking *this* is going to be our first real kiss." His eyes lit with mischief.

I wanted to tell him to shut the fuck up, but fusing our mouths together would accomplish the same thing.

And it did.

He thrust his tongue into my mouth with little preamble, and I raked my teeth along the length as I pressed my pelvis against his. His hips flexed, bringing us closer together. Reminding me I had a job to do. Sometimes the journey was as important as the destination. Today was not one of those days. Today I needed into him as quickly as I could, and I really needed him to come as quickly as he could. A passing concern about his physical health flitted through my head, but I quickly dismissed it. He'd been coherent through dinner, had drunk plenty of fluids, and very clearly knew what he wanted now.

I intended to give it to him.

I pulled back, he growled, and I grinned. I snagged the condom and wasted little time sheathing myself. I snagged the lube and coated my fingers.

He rolled his eyes.

"What?"

"I don't need prepping."

Perhaps not. Maybe he just liked it to go fast and hard. Sometimes I did as well. But tonight was not one of those nights. I wanted him to feel cared for. To know he was treasured. To get the sense he was important to me. Because he was. He was fucking everything to me.

As if sensing my steely resolve, he grabbed his knees and pulled his legs back and out of the way, affording me a lovely view.

I stroked his cock with one hand while I stuck my index finger into his entrance.

Our gazes held as I gauged every nuance. I stroked—he bit his lip. I slid in another finger—his pupils dilated. I scissored—he grunted. I hit his prostate—he let out a keening wail.

"More. God, Dickens, please, more. Want you in me. Now."

His words were vaguely coherent, but the hectic color in his cheeks made it clear I was doing a good job edging him. Mimicking his earlier action, I slid my thumb across his slit, picking up a drop of precum, and then slipped the digit into my mouth and sucked.

He bucked.

Good.

I withdrew my fingers, and he snarled.

"Down, boy. I'll give you what you want." As I coated my sheathed cock with lube, I held his gaze. I guided myself to him and tilted my head.

He nodded.

I pressed in.

He bore down.

I slid in to the hilt.

He gasped.

A moment passed where I held myself still, gazing down into his beautiful dark eyes. Then he slid his hands down my flank and grasped my ass.

I knew. Yes, he was giving me the signal to go ahead and fuck him, but he was also conveying so much more. Trust. Affection. Caring.

Dare I say...love?

He flexed his hips, drawing me in even farther. "Please." A hoarse whisper.

This I could give him. I pulled out almost to the tip and slid back in.

His fingers flexed against my ass.

Okay, message received. The next thrust was harder, and then I began a relentless pace. I didn't give him time to catch his breath, and my own grip on sanity slipped with each stroke. Faster. I needed to go faster. I needed to bring him along with me and, fuck almighty, I needed him to go over first.

I reached down to grasp his cock, but he batted my hand away.

"I'll do it."

Okay, then. Meant I could focus on wringing every ounce of pleasure out of him. Out of myself. Out of where our bodies were joined so intimately.

His jerks became frantic movements as he chased his orgasm, and he managed to grit out an, "I'm coming," just before he erupted. His cum covered his stomach and chest and a bit hit me as well. His ass gripped my cock, and that was the beginning of the end for me as well.

Several deep and violent thrusts later, I tipped over the edge myself. Into bliss. Into heaven. Into somewhere I wanted to stay forever. So many words remained unspoken.

And yet, as I collapsed onto him, everything was crystal clear.

Chapter Ten

Fritz

I awoke alone, but that didn't surprise me. I remembered, somewhere near dawn, Dickens pressing a kiss to my forehead, saying he needed to get home, mumbling something, then slipping away. I'd have sworn he said he loved me, but that was just my sleep-addled brain speaking.

Rolling out of bed, I took stock. I glanced over to my garbage can. Three used condoms, nicely tied off. The man was obsessively neat. How many times had he risen to wet a washcloth and then returned to wipe me down? Enough so I wasn't sticky despite the multiple orgasms.

I stripped the bed, even though what I really wanted to do was sink back into the dirty sheets and revel in his scent. I was attracted to everything about him. His looks, his quirky sense of humor, his caring nature...and, most especially, his scent. Something about it kicked my libido into high gear, and I sported a semi as I tossed the sheets into the laundry and headed to the shower.

The analog clock read eight forty-five, so I had enough time for a quick wash and a hearty breakfast before I headed down to open the shop.

Forty-seven minutes later, all of two minutes behind schedule, I rounded to the front of the store and found a woman standing at the door. "I apologize. Let me open up, and then please, come inside."

Before I could even unlock the door, she thrust a paper into my hand.

"This is my resumé. I have a bookkeeping background, and before I had kids, I worked at the bookstore. The Lawrences were great people—are great people—and I didn't want to quit working, but my husband said it wasn't proper for his wife to work, and then, you know, two kids, and...well, now they're in school and my husband is, uh, between jobs and—"

I held up my hand. "Why don't we take this inside?" I met her gaze as she finally looked at me. Pretty green eyes, with a delicate white face surrounded by a riot of auburn curls. She was barely an inch or two over five feet, so I literally towered over her.

She bobbed her head and her curls bobbed as well.

I unlocked the door, cringing that I hadn't set the alarm yesterday. Yet everything looked in order. I didn't have cash in the place, and the computer wasn't new either.

The motorcycles were secured and everything was fine.

Downtown Mission City was a pretty safe place, so I was good. I guided Darlene to the back room. I had set up two desks with chairs and another chair across from my desk. Trying to look like the boss I wanted to be.

I encouraged the woman to sit in the chair across from me. I sat and glanced over her resumé. Her name leapt off the top line, and as I skimmed, I found other words I recognized. Truth was, it didn't matter that I couldn't read the thing properly in a brief span of time. If Dickens trusted her, I was going to as well.

I placed the paper down on the desk. "When can you work, and when can you start?"

She straightened and pushed a lock of flyaway hair out of her face. "I can start tomorrow. I can work Mondays and Thursdays."

Perfect. I could have my Mondays off and play Thursday by ear. "That's great." I named a salary I knew I could afford.

Her eyes widened.

I was verging on panic, but then she spoke.

"That's very generous. I promise I'll work hard to earn it."

In my heart, I had no doubt. I pointed to the other desk with the computer. "I'll get you passwords. If you don't like the software, let me know, and I'll buy you whatever you want, within reason. You'll need to keep an eye on the front of the shop when you're alone."

More head bobbing. "I won't let you down."

"I never had a worry. I believe there's some paperwork you need to fill out—"

Another nod. "I know which forms. I'll print them out tonight and bring them in."

"Great. I'm trying to go entirely digital. Paper just messes with my mind."

"I understand you have some records needing to be organized. Was that correct?"

Damn interfering Dickens. "Yes, that would be correct."

She clapped her hands. "Great, just hand me the pile tomorrow, and I promise I'll get it all organized." She rose and stuck out her hand.

I grasped it. Her smile was genuine, but I didn't miss the shadows in her eyes. I shook her hand.

"Thank you so much. For all of it." She bobbed her head one last time and headed out of the office. Unsure whether to see her out or let her figure things out for herself, I let her go. I leaned back in my chair and said a silent thanks to the interfering shit next door.

The man I was coming to love. I should've panicked at that thought. I barely knew him. Yet he was so much more than Bookstore Dude now. He was Dickens. My lover. My friend.

After a moment of reflection and letting the thought settle, I headed back to the work area.

The clouds overhead blocked the sun, and the wind blew from the west.

I checked the weather forecast. Ah, rain and thunderstorms were predicted. Perfect. I was protected from the harsher elements, and could get my work done without getting heat exhaustion.

I worked diligently until my stomach rumbled.

Noon.

I stretched as I rose. Kendra's motorcycle was ready to go, and I had several buyers lined up to take her for a spin. I also had called a guy selling a classic Harley.

A few questions had him opening up on his reasons for selling. A Parkinson's diagnosis meant driving his baby just wasn't possible. But he wanted her to go to someone who'd love her.

I gave him a general overview of my enthusiastic young buyer and he said he was sure we could make a deal.

A pretty productive morning.

Now, though, I was ravenous. I locked up the work area and headed to the bathroom so I could relieve myself and scrub the grease off my hands. I didn't do a bad job, but I didn't want dirty nails. Except Dickens knew who I was. I was a mechanic and damn proud of it.

I flipped the closed sign in the window and headed out, locking the front door as I went. I eyed up and down First Avenue and landed on the exact store I sought. Within a few minutes I had what I wanted, and now I debated what to get for lunch. Had Dickens eaten? Would he want me to show up with food? Was I being too presumptuous?

Fuck it.

I grabbed a bagel with cream cheese and a BLT from Tim Horton's and headed back down to our shops. I didn't make it ten steps before I felt the first drops of rain. I hurried, but not fast enough, and within moments, the skies opened up, and the rain pounded down.

Crap. Crap. Crap.

The food was in a paper bag that would break if I didn't get it out of the rain soon. I sprinted the rest of the way, staying under awnings whenever possible. By the time I got to The Owl's Nest, I was soaked. I threw myself inside and shut the door against the blowing wind.

A giggle drew my attention.

I stood, sopping wet, just inside the door of the shop. I didn't dare take another step, lest I spread the wet to the beautiful books.

Sunshine met my gaze and held up a finger. She disappeared into the back room, and before I registered her departure, she was back with a towel. She removed the bag of food from my hands, and I grasped the towel gratefully. I rubbed at my hair, my beard, and my face. The rest of my clothes were soaked, but nothing to be done about that now. It'd all dry. Fortunately the air conditioner had been turned off, so the store was a pleasant temperature without being stuffy.

Sunshine stuck her nose into the bag. "Oh, BLT. Lovely. Dickens's favorite."

"I, uh, wasn't sure if he'd eaten."

She shook her head. "He's been in the back room diligently working on something all morning. I've been tending the store." Her blue eyes lit. "Darlene told me you've hired her." She pressed a hand to her chest. "Thank you for that. I was worried, but couldn't say anything."

"Well, she's qualified, and Dickens recommended her." As if this were the most natural thing in the world.

A wistful expression crossed the young woman's face. "Not everyone is so understanding about limitations." To my puzzled expression, she elaborated. "Limited hours. Having kids. You know, stuff."

I chuckled. "Oh, you mean life? I'm good with working around life." I sniffed. "And thank you for closing up yesterday."

An easy shrug. "I knew you'd overdone it, but that you'd be okay. I just didn't realize how truly fine you would turn out to be."

Her tone carried no licentiousness, but it left me with no doubt what she referred to. "He told you?"

She grinned. "He didn't have to. Written all over the dear man's face. Plus—" She pointed to my left hand. "—I'd say you enjoyed yourself as well."

I'd forgotten I had brought the gift for Dickens. "Over the top?"

"Never." She winked. "Let me go get him." Without leaving me time to comment, she headed back through the door.

I passed the towel over my head again, although I wasn't sure it made any difference. Before I could opine about my state of dampness, Dickens appeared.

He held something small and black in his hand. He spotted me and stopped.

"Sunshine," he muttered.

"Uh, no, Spike."

His grin was slow and steady. "No, Fritz."

My cheeks flamed. "It's Spike."

"Sure, when you're in the shop and with your biker persona, okay. But when it's just the two of us? You're going to honor your mother and let me call you Fritz."

A warm glow started in my chest and soon climbed through my torso and out to my limbs. That feeling alone could dry all my damp bits.

He indicated my hand. "Are those for Sunshine, for me, or for someone else?"

My flush intensified, and I tried to shove my hand behind my back.

He moved swiftly, grabbing my elbow.

After a moment, I relented. "For you." I shoved the bouquet of yellow carnations at him. "I know yellow means something, and I could've asked the nice guy, but I didn't want to guess and then, well, I knew red roses meant love, and it's too soon for that, right? But not for flowers. At least I don't think so. Because I need you to know how amazing last night was. How amazing you are. And, like—"

This time he moved just as swiftly. He grabbed the back of my neck, twisted my hair in his hands, and yanked me down for a kiss.

Although momentarily stunned, I recovered quickly. I pulled him against me and gave myself over to his skillful mouth.

Our tongues parried, he sought the recesses of my mouth, and then he thrust his hard cock against my belly.

Holy Lord.

I wanted to keep going. I wanted time to spin out, and for the universe to stop so we could just stay wrapped in each other's arms. The crinkling of plastic brought me out of the trance. "Your flowers." I eyed the bouquet, worried our exertions had damaged it. By all appearances, though, it'd weathered the storm.

Dickens eased back and his blue eyes sparkled. "And Sun said something about food...?"

I guffawed. "Glad to know where your priorities are."

He snagged the bouquet from my willing hands. He sniffed. "Yellow means friendship and joy." He tweaked my nose. "I think they're perfect."

I kissed his nose. "I think you're perfect. Look, I'm going to run upstairs and get into dry clothes."

"I could come with you." He waggled his brows suggestively. So different from the man I'd met mere days ago.

"If you do that, we'll never eat, I'll never get my shop open after lunch, and Sunshine will know everything."

His laugh was a joyous sound. "Sunshine already knows everything. But you're right about propriety. Get changed while I heat our food. We can eat in the back room while Sun watches the store."

I moved toward the front, but he snagged my arm. "Use the back alley."

He was right, of course. Both our entrances were covered. Less chance of getting soaked again.

"Oh, and..." He pressed the small black device into my hand.

Examining it, I squinted.

"It's one of the original iPods. Like, sixth generation or something. So much storage. I spent the morning downloading audiobooks for you. As many Harvard Classics as I could get hold of, plus tons of other stuff. Like Harry Potter, James Patterson, Stephen King, Nora Roberts..."

"Nora who?" I'd heard of the others, but not her.

Dickens grinned. "She writes romances. Our library has a bunch of gay romances, and I've added those as well. You've got several hundred hours of listening. Like literally days worth."

This was, without question, the nicest gift anyone'd ever given me. My eyes watered.

"No." He moaned. "I didn't want to make you cry."

"Happy tears, I promise." I angled my head down, he tipped his chin up, and we met for a tender kiss. "This is the best present ever."

"That's a pretty high bar for me to set, my first time out." He grazed my beard with his index finger. "But I'm creative. I'll find ways to top it."

"But you don't need to," I protested.

"Oh, yes, I do." He propelled me toward the back door and smacked my ass. "Get changed and let's eat. I'm starving."

As I passed through the door, Sunshine appeared and stopped directly before me. "I knew."

Where I expected smugness, there was only deep contentment.

The woman was happy for her boss. Was happy for me.

In that moment, I wished she might one day find the same happiness.

Without another word, I bolted outside and sprinted up the stairs. The quicker I changed, the quicker I could head back downstairs and spend time with my new man.

Epilogue

Dickens

The day Isaac walked back into my life was the day I proposed to Fritz.

I should explain. Fritz and I'd been dating almost six months. We spent every night at my place and we'd even—slowly—talked about getting a house together. And a dog. For sure a dog. But we'd either wait until Ari passed or—since the cat appeared to be going strong—we'd find a dog who loved cats.

Ari'd met many pooches who came into the store over the years and she never fussed. She looked at them, they looked at her, and everyone went on with their lives.

I wondered how she'd handle a full-time canine companion. Knowing my little one? Probably with aplomb.

Anyway, it'd been on my mind to propose to Fritz, and then Isaac walked through the door of my shop. I was stunned speechless. He was just as beautiful as I remembered.

Dark skin, soulful brown eyes, and a shy smile.

But where my heart used to speed up, it maintained a normal rhythm. Where I used to feel bone-deep attraction, I felt only warm comfort. He'd been a friend as well as a lover and, in that moment, I hoped we could be friendly again. He'd broken my heart, but it'd been first love. Now, with the benefit of hindsight, I saw what I had with Fritz went so much deeper. True love. Forever companionship. 'Til-death-do-us-part shit.

"Hello, Dickens."

His voice was even deeper than I remembered. I stepped out from behind the counter and offered my hand.

He grabbed it and pulled me in for a hug.

It felt good. Like releasing tension I'd carried for half-a-dozen years.

After a bit, he pulled back and ducked his head.

"I'm happy to see you." I gave him my most genuine smile.

"Are you?"

"Yes." I offered the word enthusiastically.

He scratched his bald head. "Well, that's good because, well, I've taken the job as harbor master here in Mission City."

Stunned speechless. He came from landlocked Whitehorse. But now he wanted to be near the water?

"I can see I've surprised you." He grinned ruefully. "I've spent the past three years working the lighthouse in Tofino. That was great, but too far from the city. I figure being in Mission City will give me the small-town feeling, but I can head to Vancouver whenever the feeling hits me."

"And Davie Street?" The local hangout for gay men.

His eyes widened. "Well, sure, if Ben is up for it."

"Ben?"

"Ben Whitaker."

I wracked my brains. I'd heard the name. Nice guy. Several years younger than me. Elementary school teacher? French Immersion, if memory served. Hadn't realized he was gay, but that wasn't a huge surprise.

"So you're moving to Mission City because of Ben?"

His grin was rueful. "I agreed to take the position and then met Ben. Things all came together. Now, I wasn't sure he wanted a relationship after our weekend fling but..." Despite his dark skin, a blush emerged.

"Well, this is great news. I'd love to introduce you to my..." I floundered. Fritz and I had never named our relationship. We hadn't needed to. We were together. Practically lived together. Worked side by side literally. Hell, I'd even learned to live with the motorcycle engine noise. "...partner?"

"Dickens, that sounded like a question." His eyes twinkled in amusement.

In that moment, everything became clear. "I'm going to ask him to marry me. And I don't know if he'll say yes, but..." I flapped my hand. So unlike me.

"I'm sure he'll say yes. Or he will if he has any sense." A wistful expression passed over Isaac's face. "If we'd stayed together, then I never would've met Ben."

"And I wouldn't have met Fritz. You see, it was all meant to be."

"Yeah." He scratched his head again. "So we're good?"

"We're more than good." I offered an impish smile. "We're friends."

A matching grin. "I like that. I can use more friends in this town." He gave a little wave and headed back outside into the nippy air.

Christmas was just around the corner.

Sunshine breezed into the room, her green corduroy jumper with Santa's grinning face matching a swishy skirt of the same fabric. She stopped, gave me one long level look and asked, "Did you buy him a ring?"

"Uh..."

"And you have to be creative."

"Dare I ask?"

"Oh, you'll figure it out." She made a shooing motion. "Now, go find something nice. Something strong that he can wear at work."

"I don't mind if he takes it off while he works." Honestly, Fritz didn't need a ring. Neither did I. This commitment we had transcended symbols.

"Yeah, whatever, make it a good one. Oh, I know a jeweler in Vancouver. You'll love her."

I eyed the threatening storm clouds.

The meteorologists predicted first snow of the year.

"You'll be fine." She placed her hand on her hip. "Now, go."

So I did. Made the round trip to Vancouver in just under three hours. The snow started about halfway home, and by the time I pulled into Mission City, I was sweating under the strain of driving in the snow. One of my least favorite things to do. I drove past my store to find it shuttered for the night. Oh, good, Sun had left early.

The light in Spike's shop was still on, but he'd be closing up soon.

I parked around back and sprinted up to my apartment. I hopped into the shower to wash off the gross stress sweat and then lay down on the bed. I positioned the ring perfectly and snapped a picture, then sent it to Fritz's phone.

Forty-two seconds later, his heavy footfalls clomped up the stairs. He burst through the door and slammed it shut. Two thuds as he so considerately removed his boots. Within moments, he was at the threshold to my bedroom.

He held up his phone.

I grinned.

He sputtered. "You sent me a dick pic."

"Well, given my name is Dickens, I would say it's about time."

Slowly, he crept into the room, peering over to hone in on my crotch.

My erection lay heavy against my belly and a drop of precum leaked onto the ring which lay just below my navel.

"You sent me a dick pic." His voice carried a note of wonder.

"I'm also proposing. Keep your eye on the prize. Or should I say the ring?"

Our gazes met. I read the uncertainty, and it hurt my heart. Because it wasn't uncertainty about me, but uncertainty about himself. Over and over, during the last six months, I'd tried to convince him I didn't care about what he couldn't do.

He'd gone so far as to hire a tutor to help him improve his reading.

I knew how hard he tried. I couldn't convince him I didn't need him in any way other than the way he was. He was perfect. He was my perfect.

Slowly, he advanced into the room. He eased onto the bed and sat so our hips touched. With exquisite gentleness, he ran his hand from my knee, up my thigh, and across my hipbone to my navel. Reverently, he touched the ring.

"Try it on."

He did.

To my infinite relief, it fit.

He held up his hand, and the light glinted off the platinum. "Did you get one for yourself?"

I'd spent the entire trip into town debating and the entire trip home waffling between certainty and regret. Finally, I relented. "Top drawer of my nightstand."

He leaned over to open it and pulled out the box. He flipped it open and grasped the ring. Matching in every way. "I should've done this."

"Impulse buy."

His expression darkened.

Crap.

"Not buying your ring." I snagged his hand. "That was a no-brainer. I wasn't sure whether to buy one for myself, but I want everyone to know we're together—"

"I don't think there's a resident in Mission City who doesn't know."

"Still..." I squeezed his hand. "If it's too soon, we can tuck them away."

His fist closed around the ring. "No way. Your parents are coming for Christmas. Can we marry then?"

I sputtered. "Like, in two weeks?"

"Yes." Absolute certainty.

My parents had visited several times since June, and they loved Fritz. My mother loved to feed him, and my father liked to pretend he was interested in getting a motorcycle. At least I hoped he was feigning interest. My mother'd kill him if he actually bought one.

"Sure, Fritz, if that's what you want."

"I do."

Insane for me, though. His business was virtually dead, while I was in the middle of the craziest time of the year. But, for him, I'd do anything. "Okay, let me make some calls."

His grin went from ear to ear. Slowly, he slid the ring onto my finger. Of course it fit perfectly. "I love you. I know I say it all the time, but I need to say it again."

"And I echo the sentiment all the time, but sometimes I'm not sure you believe me." I pushed myself up so I could take his cheeks in my hands. "I love you, Fritz. I always have, and I always will."

"Even with my terrible taste in music and my love of loud engines?"

I grinned in return. "I heard you playing *Living on a Prayer* yesterday."

He shrugged. "Great song."

My hands went to his jean shirt, and I started to unbutton it.

He hadn't been working in the shop today, so there wasn't any grease on his hands.

Not that I ever cared. He was what mattered.

Later, as we lay tangled in each other's arms, he snuggled against my neck. "So we're agreed on a house?"

"We are."

"And we're agreed about a dog?"

"If Ari is amenable." At the moment, my cat was curled up on her favorite chair in the living room. We spent our time here, as opposed to Fritz's place, so my little girl was never alone.

"What about kids?" His voice was tentative.

We probably should've had this conversation *before* getting engaged.

"I love Darlene's kids, but they don't make me want to have some of my own." I pulled back to gaze at him. "I know it will disappoint my parents, but I don't think having kids to give them grandchildren is a good plan."

"Oh, thank God." He wiped the sweat from his brow.

"You're okay with not having kids?" I suspected I now knew the answer, but I needed confirmation.

"Kids are so much work. And I love other people's kids, but I don't want to take on that responsibility. I want to keep volunteering, but that's enough." He helped at a charity that fixed up donated bikes and gave them to kids whose parents couldn't afford them. A brilliant use of his talents.

"Then we're good." I placed a kiss to his forehead. "This is a forever thing. You get that, right?"

"I do."

And two weeks later, before my parents, our friends, and match-maker Sunshine, we repeated that vow to each other.

Want to know about Dickens's ex-boyfriend, Isaac? Turn the page and see his story...

The Lightkeeper's Love Affair

A Mission City Gay Romance Short Story

Gabbi Grey

Dedication

Randall

Cate

B^{en}

I just graduated. I should be out celebrating. Instead, a storm's coming and I've got no to place to sleep except the backseat of my car. At least I have my beloved beagle with me, but seriously, how is this my life?

Isaac

After a horrific week, I hate being unable to retreat to my island sanctuary. Perhaps sharing my hotel room with a stranger in distress and his dog will take my mind off things. Afterward, we'll separate and never meet again. Right?

*A 10k lighthearted gay romance with forced proximity, a loner, a future school-teacher, and Buddy, the adorable beagle. This short story was originally published in the anthology Ukraine: Seeds of Love.

Contents

Chapter One

Ben

What the actual fuck?

The hotel desk clerk held my gaze with a level look, her hazel eyes scrutinizing me.

Buddy rubbed against my leg.

I did mental gymnastics. "Does that come with food?"

"Complimentary breakfast buffet." She patted her platinum blonde hair in its elegant chignon.

Ugh, too similar to my mother. None of the scenarios in my mind appealed. The storm that'd been threatening my entire trip up from Nanaimo had finally materialized—part of the reason my poor beagle was cowering by my legs.

So a return trip back to the ferry was out. And likely the ferry back to Vancouver would be canceled due to the high winds anyway. Authorities were threatening to close the highways.

My friend Marisa was never going to make it down here.

Damn woman.

This'd been her idea. Graduation celebration in Tofino. Winter surfing before we started our teaching careers in January. Who the hell surfed in early December? In the middle of storm season on Vancouver Island? My best friend, apparently. With whom I was supposed to be sharing the room. Sharing the expense. Eighteen months of teacher's college had me completely tapped out.

I laid my head on the counter, revelling in the cool of the granite.

"You know I'd help if I could, Isaac."

The other desk clerk's quiet voice carried through my panic.

"I'll call around to see if there's somewhere else." He sounded doubtful.

"It's okay, I can search myself. I just hoped to get home today and now it looks like I'm stuck for a few days."

This guy was also in a predicament, I presumed.

"You do hate to be landlocked." The soft-spoken clerk again.

I glanced over at the Black man putting his wallet away. Surely there must be plenty of rooms available. This was the off-season. In Tofino. My gaze returned to the woman. "He can have my room."

The man cleared his throat.

She arched a brow.

"We can, you know, sleep in my car. And head back out in the morning." I looked down at Buddy.

The man moved toward me, and I turned to face him.

"This storm is the first of three atmospheric rivers headed this way. It's likely they'll close the highway in case of flooding. You're pretty much stuck." His voice was a soothing baritone.

"I can't be stuck." I gazed back and forth between the clerk and the man who had a good four inches on me. "There's got to be a cheaper place. Or maybe I can head out before the road closes."

"And stay where? The ferry terminal?" His brow creased.

"We have two weddings booked this weekend, but, as Mike said, we can call around to find other accommodation for you both." The officious clerk's arched eyebrow didn't move.

The man pulled out his credit card. "We're two adult men. We can manage a room together."

He met my gaze as I tried not to gape.

"At least if you don't mind sharing your room. I have no problem paying." As he said the words, another lash of rain hit the front door.

This couldn't be happening.

And yet it was.

Deal with it.

"Uh, yeah. I mean, thank you. I can pay half." Again, with the gymnastic calculations. I taught French Immersion to elementary school children, so I usually needed only basic arithmetic.

His smile was genuine, and he showed me his perfect teeth. "I get to put the expense on the company card."

"Well, in that case, sign me up."

He handed his card to the overbearing desk clerk.

She smiled far more benevolently than anything she'd given me. Apparently she knew the guy because a minute later she handed him a paper to sign.

I tried to glance at the signature, but couldn't see it. Hadn't the other clerk said the guy's name was Isaac? "Oh, are you okay with dogs?" A little late to be asking.

Instead of responding, the man crouched down to Buddy's level. "Hello, little one, my name is Isaac." He held out his hand, palm down, knuckles bent.

I held my breath as I waited. My rescue dog sometimes was gregarious and accepting, but other times he was nervous and withdrawn.

Buddy leaned over as far as his little body could go, took a good sniff, eyed Isaac warily, and finally nudged with his cute little black-button nose.

Isaac giggled. Yes, the grown man giggled. Then he tipped his head back to meet my gaze. "I think we're going to be okay." He rose and accepted the two key cards the woman handed him. He immediately gave one to me.

"Room 303," she said. "Ocean view."

"Not much to see," I muttered, gazing out at the pouring rain.

"I'll show you when things calm down. There'll be lulls."

I was dubious at this point, but willing to accept what Isaac said. I snagged my rolling suitcase, and he hefted his rucksack. With a click of my tongue to signal Buddy, the three of us headed to the elevator. This was going to be the longest three days of my life.

Chapter Two

Isaac

I was so grateful the longest week of my life was at an end, I wasn't even going to stress about not getting back to my home.

My other home.

The past week in my hometown burying my grandfather was an experience I was so happy I'd never have to repeat. The vicious old man'd been pretty much my only living relative, and now that he was safely in the earth, I could breathe. I'd inhaled a great lungful of air in Whitehorse, Yukon as I waited for the plane that'd bring me back to Vancouver. I'd stood on the deck of the ferry and inhaled the sea air as we made our way from the town of Tsawwassen on the mainland to Swartz Bay in Nanaimo on Vancouver Island. I'd rolled down my window and let the cold winter air blow through my car as I drove to Tofino. To the only home I'd known for the past three years.

Now, though, the last leg of my journey was stymied. Just a boat ride. One brief boat ride out to Lennard Island. There I could stand on the edge of the cliff, breathe freely, and then settle back into my routine. And let my replacement take her well-earned time off.

Veronica covered me without a moment's hesitation, but she had family to return to. She was on maternity leave, but said she needed a break from her seven-month-old son and her big lug of a husband. He needed to step up, since she'd be back at work in a few months. Her rotations would keep her away for one or two weeks a month, and he had to learn to cope without her.

Personally, I didn't think he was up for the task, but maybe he'd matured with the birth of their son. I could hope.

And now these storms were delaying Ronnie's return.

As if I needed even more guilt for interrupting her break.

The elevator ride was quick, and soon we found ourselves in front of room 303.

I swiped my card and pushed the door open, holding it so...shit, I didn't even know the guy's name...and Buddy could enter. I flipped on the lights because we needed them.

Three o'clock in the afternoon, and the room was shrouded in darkness. Little light came from the window.

I stopped short.

One bed.

Oh my God, this was every cheesy romance book I'd ever read. Two people. One bed. Forced to stay the night together. I should've let Mike find me another place. Except the lodge was on the list of approved accommodations, so I didn't have to go through a lengthy process. I handed them my government card, and everything was arranged.

The guy handed me Buddy's leash. "I gotta go."

Go where? I recovered quickly as he dashed to the washroom. Ah, long drive from the ferry across the island. I knew this and had planned accordingly.

Buddy gazed up at me with soulful brown eyes. Beseeching me to...what? I'd never had a dog growing up. Then I was living in residence at the university. After that, back to Whitehorse until I couldn't live with that hateful bigot any longer, and so I left on a string of assignments. I could get a dog now, but that'd mean more provisions to bring over to the island, and what if she didn't like boats?

The flushing toilet pulled me back from wherever I'd gone. I unclipped Buddy's leash, and he eyed me warily before planting his nose to the carpet and beginning his exploration.

The lodge had a number of pet-friendly rooms. Despite the care and diligence of the cleaning staff, ridding the room of all canine and feline scents would be impossible.

As I tossed my rucksack into the closet, the guy emerged.

"Yeah, so my name is Ben—Benjamin. Whitaker." His blue eyes sparkled. "Okay, like, just please don't call me Benjy."

"Would never have dreamed of doing so." I held out my hand. "I'm Isaac."

He accepted it immediately. "Yeah, the guy said it. Cool name."

I didn't think so, but okay. I indicated his suitcase and pointed to the corner. Then I pointed to the closet.

His gaze settled on the bed. "Oh."

"Yes." I cleared my throat. "No big deal. I mean, we're both grown adults."

"I might snore."

I tilted my head. "Might?"

"Yeah. I mean, my last boyfriend said I did, and I think he was just saying it to, like, piss me off, you know? He was a bit of a jerk." He ran his hand through his brown hair. "No, he was a lot of a jerk. But he was a PhD student and so freaking smart that I just...well, you know...and with him being gay and..." His eyes widened. "Oh, crap. I mean, I probably should've said something before, right? I mean, you don't seem like a homophobic type, but you might, I dunno, have religious beliefs or—"

"Or I might be gay myself."

I'd heard the expression *jaw dropping to the floor*, but I couldn't remember ever witnessing it to quite such an exacting degree. Of course, his chin didn't hit the floor, but his mouth gaped open.

Oh, this was going to be fun.

Chapter Three

Ben

Okay, so math wasn't my strong suit, but I still tried to calculate the odds of me winding up here, in this town, in this lodge, on this day, and having to share a room with the most handsome guy I'd met in a while *and* he was gay?

Astronomical came to mind.

Or today was the luckiest day of my life. Right up there with the day I got into teacher's college. About the same odds, I figured.

Isaac cleared his throat. "So we've discovered there are no homophobes in the room. That's a good thing." He squinted. "And I don't really care one way or the other, but do you snore? I'm pretty sure I'll sleep like the dead tonight after the insane week I've had, but I can request ear plugs just in case."

I flushed. "I think the guy was just saying that. He tossed tons of insults my way. Jackass." And I so did not want to be thinking about him at this moment. "Do you snore?"

"No one's ever complained, but it's been a few years since I shared a bed with anyone."

Did that mean he just had sex and left, or did it mean he hadn't been with anyone?

"I've been celibate for almost five years."

Holy shit.

Okay, question answered. I hadn't gone more than four months without sex since I started experimenting at sixteen. I figured out how to find guys pretty easily, living in Vancouver and all. Lately, it'd been more challenging since I was living in Abbotsford, the bible belt of the Fraser Valley, and attending the local university. Within spitting range of Vancouver, but a pain in my ass to do all that driving when I was supposed to be studying. And I was moving next week to Mission City where I was starting at my new school, Cedar Street Elementary, after Christmas. A teacher was going on maternity leave, and the school had leapt on my application. Done deal.

I gazed at my new roommate. Dark skin, bright dark-brown eyes, and a shaved head. A head he kept scratching.

He noted my interest. "I started going bald when I turned twenty-four. Not wanting to look dorky, I opted to start shaving my head. I'm overdue. Been kind of busy."

"Doing what, if you don't mind me asking?" Which was way too personal, but we had about an hour to kill until dinnertime.

Another head scratch. "Burying my grandfather. He died two weeks ago, and since I was the only remaining relative, the job fell to me. I took the time off work and went up to Whitehorse. Pretty straightforward. Guy didn't have many friends, and he rented a run-down shack just outside of town. I gave away anything of value, hauled the rest to the dump, saw him buried, and headed back here."

Wow, that sounded so sad. Except he didn't look sad. He looked...neutral? Or maybe just tired. Everyone handled grief differently. I'd be devastated if one of my grandfathers died. Both were in their seventies, so that possibility definitely existed. I wouldn't have them forever. But hopefully a while longer yet. "Do you want to watch television or something?"

A small smile. "I'm good. I have some weather reports to read." He walked over to the desk, scooped up the remote, and handed it to me.

Our fingers brushed.

He'd done that on purpose, right? Because the thing was big enough, we didn't need to touch.

You're overthinking this. He handed you the remote. Thank him. Move on.

"Thanks. I'll keep the volume down."

"No worries, Ben. I'm able to focus."

He said my name in such a soothing dulcet tone. It washed over me like a gentle wave.

Finally breaking eye contact, he headed over to his rucksack, pulled out a laptop and a power cord, and then headed over to the desk.

Still, I stood like an idiot.

He gave me a quick look before sitting in the desk chair and getting settled.

Rain lashed across the window.

I headed over that way.

The day was gray and dark, with the clouds hanging low. The rain pelted sideways in the strong winds.

The ocean side of Vancouver Island sometimes saw hurricane-force winds, and I wondered if we might today. Why hadn't I checked the forecast?

Because Marisa said she'd take care of it.

Why hadn't I called her?

Because she said she'd be here.

Marisa lived up near Campbell River and had gone home for a couple of days. She was supposed to meet me here. We were going to surf, then we were scheduled to head back to school for some wrap-up sessions. But exams were over. We were essentially finished.

Marisa had secured a job teaching in her old hometown, and her parents were thrilled.

I was under the distinct impression she was not. I didn't see how she'd survive being back in a small town, but she was a big girl. And if she didn't like it, she could join me.

Not that Mission City was big. But its proximity to Vancouver offered plenty of options. Campbell River was in the middle of Vancouver Island. Basically, the middle of nowhere.

I yanked my phone from my back pocket.

Finally.

An apology text from her. Blathering on about how she'd been too busy to check the weather reports, and now her parents wouldn't drive her down to Tofino and how the first thing she was buying with her first paycheck was a car...

I typed out a simple *all good* and left it at that. I wasn't going to tell her about Isaac. The woman was way too good at ferreting out personal details of my life I never intended to share. I eyed my new roommate. Well, at least he was pretty to look at.

Chapter Four

Isaac

The low hum of the television sat in my consciousness. I stared at the meteorological charts and winced.

Three storms in a continuous line from Hawaii all the way to southern British Columbia. The second one had been veering south of us toward Washington State, but the trajectory changed an hour ago and was now on a path to hit the west side of Vancouver Island and Vancouver's lower mainland.

November had been unusually dry, but much of British Columbia had been scorched during the summer wildfires. That combination meant unstable ground and the likelihood of landslides. Between that and the anticipated gale-force winds, we weren't going anywhere.

Even if things calmed enough between storms for me to get out to the island, Ronnie would be taking the risk on the return journey. No, better to wait.

An email from headquarters in my inbox assured me she was fine. She'd weathered storms this bad before and would likely again.

The intensity seemed to grow every year. Climate change. Or so they said.

I powered down the laptop and glanced at my watch. Seventeen-thirty-three. My unexpected roommate sat on the bed, propped against the headboard. I pivoted and found him watching the weather channel.

He glanced at me and raised the volume.

A shot of one of those crazy news reporters standing out in the storm, reporting on how bad the storm was. Nuts. The woman was nuts. Whoever thought *that* was a good idea? Her bosses needed to have their heads examined.

That being said, if I had an equipment failure or something like that, I'd be out as well, so maybe just...doing her job?

At the end of her segment, Ben shut off the television. "Do we go down to get food or do we order room service?"

I eyed Buddy. "There's a restaurant here that allows pets, believe it or not. Well, dogs. Not cats. And you're not supposed to feed your dog from your plate, but people do it."

Buddy perked up at his name.

He truly was adorable. "How old?"

"Eighteen months. I got him when he was six months old. Terrible situation. But now he's with me and life is great. I didn't plan to get a dog right as I was starting teacher's college, but sometimes we don't get to pick when our destiny comes along."

"Buddy is your destiny?"

Ben nodded vigorously. His mahogany hair shone in the light and he had a bit of five o'clock shadow accumulating. He was also adorable.

"Well, why don't we head downstairs?" I extended a hand to Buddy.

He cocked his head, glanced at Ben, looked back at me, and offered his paw.

"Good boy." I petted him on the head.

As a group, we headed to the stairs. Two flights down and we were back in the lobby. Ben and Buddy followed my lead as I guided them to the Paw Express restaurant. We didn't have a reservation, and in tourist season you definitely needed one, but we were okay tonight. The host pointed to the table by the huge plate-glass windows and I nodded. A perfect view out over the ocean.

We sat across from each other while Buddy tucked himself under the table.

Within moments, our server, Oana, appeared. "Hey, fancy seeing you here."

I grinned. A little forced, though. I didn't want to be here. I wanted to be over on the island.

"You landlocked?"

"Until the storms pass."

"Fair enough." She eyed Buddy and handed Ben a smaller menu.

His eyes lit as he reviewed all the options. He selected a serving of beef stew with carrots, potatoes, and peas.

"And for yourself?"

"Oh." He blushed. "Like, a burger or something. Or do you have fish?"

"We specialize in fish. How about salmon? Grilled?"

He nodded.

"I'll have the burger with extra tomatoes and no lettuce."

She winked. "Back in a jiffy."

"I thought you said I can't feed Buddy."

"From your plate," I prompted. "They'll feed him for you. Beef stew?"

"Oh, he loves it. He's going to be so spoiled." He said the last sentence in that cutesy way some owners spoke to their pets.

Usually I found it irritating. Today I found it adorable.

There was that word again.

Oana returned with a small dish of stew and two glasses of water. "You guys want anything stronger?"

I held up my hand. "I'm good."

Ben hesitated before repeating the gesture.

"You can have a drink, Ben."

He eyed me.

Disconcertingly, he seemed to see through me.

"I rarely imbibe. I overdid it a couple of nights ago when I finished my final exam."

Possibly true. Probably true. But I sensed more to the story.

He took a sip of water. "So what do you do, Isaac? When you're not landlocked, that is."

I took a sip of water. "I'm the lightkeeper at Lennard Island."

Chapter Five

Ben

Lightkeeper? At first I wasn't sure what Isaac meant, but once he started talking, it all fell into place. The guy worked in a lighthouse. Out on an island. Sometimes by himself and sometimes with an assistant. And he'd been an assistant at Egg Island and Estevan Point, both places north of here, before landing this plum assignment. He'd been here almost three years.

I had so many questions I wanted to ask, but I didn't want to seem dumb. I wasn't the brightest guy around. Especially compared to my ex. I barely squeaked into teacher's college. And that was mostly because my French was excellent and I'd put in hundreds of volunteer hours. I might not be the shiniest penny in the drawer, but kids loved me, and I loved teaching them. In the end, that was all that really mattered.

"I've talked nonstop." Isaac eyed my empty plate and his barely touched meal and shrugged ruefully.

"But you've lived this fascinating life." He'd briefly touched on living up in the Yukon as a kid and being raised in semi-wilderness with his maternal grandfather. He hadn't mentioned parents at all, and I wasn't going to broach the subject. He'd share if he felt it was important.

"So, teacher's college." He waved his fork.

"Not much to tell. Eighteen-month program. Officially finished next week. Graduation in the spring, but I get my own grade-three class starting at the beginning of January."

"Grade three, eh? Bet they'll be a handful." Finally, he took a bite of his burger.

"They're little rascals. I taught this class for a couple of weeks in the fall, so I feel like I've got a handle on them. My mentor warned me they're at their worst just before breaks."

He tilted his head in question.

"Many of the kids come from unstable homes. School is the constant in their lives. When they're facing time away from school, they're never sure what that'll bring. For some of them, school breakfast and lunch are the only guaranteed meals they get."

I didn't miss the wince.

"So, where is this placement? You said you were at the university in Abbotsford..."

"Oh, my placement is in Mission City. I'm renting an apartment, and why are you looking at me like that?"

He appeared as slack-jawed as I'd been when I found out he was gay. Still tickled pink by that revelation.

He cleared his throat. Then he scratched his head. Finally, he straightened his cloth napkin with unsteady fingers.

"Okay, what gives?" I was dying of curiosity.

"Nothing." He scratched his nose.

"No, not nothing." I tipped his chin so he met my gaze. The gesture was oddly intimate, yet in the moment, it felt right.

Our gazes held. After an interminable amount of time, he relented. "My ex-boyfriend lives in Mission City."

I whistled. "Okay, small world." I furrowed my brow. "So who's your ex? I mean, I don't know many people in town..."

"Dickens Lawrence. He works at The Owl's Nest."

"The bookstore?" I wracked my brain. "I thought he owned the store."

He tilted his head. "I hadn't heard that. But we lost touch after I went back to Whitehorse."

"But then you came back to B.C.?"

"I did, but I landed the job as assistant lightkeeper up the coast. Hardly worth calling on my ex who's way off..." He gestured vaguely eastward.

"Did it end badly?" Did I need to know this? No. Was I intensely curious? Oh, hell yes. Dickens was shorter than me, and if memory served, had blond hair with blue eyes. And cute glasses. I'd gone into the store one afternoon to browse and he'd caught my attention, but not for any discernible reason. I hadn't known he was gay, but hearing he was didn't surprise me.

"We'd started to talk about plans." He scratched his head. "I mean, we weren't always compatible, but we made things work. Then my grandfather got sick and, well, I felt I had to come home."

"And yet you didn't stay."

His rage was incandescent. "The old bastard wasn't sick. By the time I realized, Dickens and I had already parted. I tried to stick around

Whitehorse, but I got fed up with my grandfather's bullshit." He pressed a finger to his lips. "Sorry."

I made a big deal of looking down at Buddy, who was fast asleep on my feet after his beef-stew feast. "It's okay, tender ears didn't hear."

That, as I hoped, made him smile.

"I came out to my grandfather. In spectacular fashion. He told me to leave and never come back, and I was happy to go." He rubbed his eyes. "My parents died in a plane crash when I was little. My father's family was from Jamaica and my mother was from the north. The Canadian authorities didn't want to send me to the Caribbean when I had a perfectly good relative here in the country. In my heart, I doubt my mother would've wanted me to go to her father. He railed on about my 'heritage'."

He said the words with air quotes.

"You mean because you're Black?"

"Nailed it in one. My grandfather was a racist. He didn't like the Indigenous people either, and there were plenty where we lived. He was just a hateful old man."

"Are you conflicted now?"

He tilted his head.

"About his death?"

A vehement shake. "No, as far as I was concerned, he died five years ago. This week was just the burial."

He bit into his burger and I glanced out the window into the dark. We were nearly upon the winter solstice, and night came early this time of year. "Look, I need to run Buddy out. But let's do something fun tonight, okay?"

Sorrowful brown eyes lightened. "What did you have in mind?"

"Leave that up to me." With a wink, I grabbed Buddy's leash, and we headed out. Now I needed to track down supplies.

Chapter Six

Isaac

Fun?

I should've been vaguely concerned what Ben had up his sleeves, but I wasn't.

Why did I tell him all that?

Because you're feeling raw.

All that's in the past.

So you tell yourself.

I munched on the last few fries as I contemplated my life. Job I loved? Check. Sense of purpose and fulfilment? Check. Lonely as fuck? Check.

Oana brought me the slip, and I signed my room number. I'd have to pay for Ben's meals from my own pocket, but that'd be my pleasure.

Five years in lighthouses, despite the paltry salary, left me with few places to spend my money.

And my grandfather had a few hundred in his bank account that would come to me soon. Despite his continued animosity toward me, he named me next of kin. He rented that old shack and he had no possessions of value, but he had a savings account.

I shouldn't be so dismissive.

He also had a small pile of photographs of me. Each stage of development, he had a shot. Even had kept the one of my university graduation. Those, along with the three of my mother, I tucked away.

My father's family had sent me copies of photos from his time in Jamaica before coming to Canada, so I had those to cling to as well. I had no memory of them, as I'd been only two. I remembered being shuttled to the Yukon, and everything after that was unpleasant.

But the old son of a bitch raised me and helped pay for my education, so I owed him a moment's consideration.

And that moment passed rather quick.

I rose and headed out of the restaurant, noting several dogs chowing down on bowls of food or resting at their masters' feet. God, I loved this place. Feeling restless, I sprinted up the stairs and let myself into our room.

Our room.

I liked the sound of that. First time in half-a-dozen years I was sharing something with someone. Could this be more than a fling? Of course not. Mission City. Tofino. Why would he want to come and stay on an island? And I didn't get enough vacation time to make it worthwhile. No, this was a one-and-done.

I snagged my sleep pants and T-shirt and headed to the bathroom. I also nabbed my toothbrush and paste because, well, one never knew. And oral hygiene, of course.

As I exited the bathroom, Ben and Buddy entered our room. Both were soaked to the skin. I grabbed the doggie towel and, after I made eye contact with Buddy, enveloped him in a big hug with the towel.

"Oh, he loves rubdowns." Ben toed off his shoes and removed his coat, hanging it in the closet. "That'll drip dry. Good Lord."

Buddy licked my cheek as I continued to dry him. Or at least did the best I could.

"I'm going to grab a shower."

Before I could respond, Ben made a beeline for the bathroom.

Buddy followed his master with his gaze, but, after the door closed, resumed his inspection of me.

I rubbed the top of his head.

He licked my cheek again.

I wasn't sure I'd ever been so absurdly touched by such a small but significant gesture.

"You want to lie down in the bed?" I pointed to the bed with a stuffed animal.

Buddy moved toward it cautiously, sniffed, then settled with his head resting upon it.

I flicked on the gas fireplace.

It'd warm the room nicely. Not great for the environment, but nights like this were made for exceptions.

I closed the drapes and headed back toward the bed, but a paper bag caught my attention.

Had Ben brought it with him? The thing was mostly dry, so he must've acquired it after he came back inside. And when had he dropped it? Probably while I'd been focused on Buddy.

I shouldn't, but I couldn't help myself. I opened it to find a box of condoms and a bottle of lube. Now, maybe Mike wasn't working the desk, and maybe the clerk who provided these necessities wouldn't be able to put two and two together, but now a chance existed the staff knew what I'd be up to tonight.

Did I care?

No.

The lodge had a pride flag amongst their other flags from different countries around the globe. A welcome to all, they said. Including people like myself.

Ben and I'd exchanged looks over dinner. A few lingering. Enough to mean we'd be good in bed? Well, one way to find out. I yanked down the comforter and top sheet. I shed my clothes and hopped onto the bed. Finally, I removed the safety plastic from the bottle of lube, opened the box of condoms, and dropped several on the bed.

I used to be a Boy Scout, and I believed in being prepared.

The hair dryer's buzz carried through the closed door, and I had second thoughts. What if the condoms weren't meant for me? He said he was supposed to meet a friend. I thought he said a female friend. What if he was bi, and she was his girlfriend? What if—

He exited the bathroom with just a towel around his waist. He stopped short when he saw me. Naked. On the bed. Half hard.

His whistle brought reassurance, as did the wolfish grin. He glanced over at Buddy who was down for the count. Then he removed his towel, tossed it back into the bathroom, and stalked over to the bed.

Despite the fireplace, the room hadn't heated yet, and goosebumps covered my skin.

"You'll have to let me warm you up." He eased onto the mattress.

"I like the sound of that." And I did. But there was one little thing... "How, do you, you know..."

He chuckled. "I'm truly good either way. I don't want to presume, but I sort of guess you're a top and—"

I pounced, catching him off-guard, and rolling him so he was under me. "You would be correct on that score."

Be still my pounding heart. This was going to be fun.

Chapter Seven

Ben

His dark-brown eyes sparkled in the firelight. Part of me wished I could've set up candles and soft romantic music, but the rest of me understood now wasn't the time. Dinner had been foreplay. Now was the time for fun.

He pinned me down and eased over me. His soft skin, covered in goosebumps, rubbed against me. He was soft, his muscles were not. Either his job was more physical than I thought, or he worked out. Me? Not so much these days. I used to swim, and I planned to go back to that. My university friend, Quinn, was a lifeguard at the Mission City Civic pool and she was going to set me up. At this moment, though, I wished I took better care of myself. Not necessarily chiseled abs, but something harder.

Well, one part of me was definitely hard. Isaac's proximity to me, along with the fact he was a top, had me revving up. I meant it when I said it didn't matter to me. But here, in this space, it mattered a whole hell of a lot. I was willing to put myself into this man's hands. Instinctively I knew he'd cherish me. He was just that kind of guy.

He eased himself down my body, making sure our skin was in constant contact.

Ripples of desire rolled through me as I held my breath, waiting for his next move. He didn't make me wait long, as he knelt between my thighs.

He grasped my length.

I nearly bucked.

His fingers explored as he pulled back my foreskin.

A drop of precum pooled at the tip.

He met my gaze.

I nodded.

He swept up the moisture with his tongue.

I moaned as I absorbed the abrasion of his tongue against my sensitive slit. I swore I saw stars.

As he swirled my head in his mouth, little jolts of electricity shot through me. I'd had guys go down on me before, but it'd never felt this intimate. Like we shared some secret. Here in this room by ourselves.

The storm enclosed us in this little bubble of tranquility.

I heard the trees lashing against the window, but I felt protected. Nothing would ever touch me. Not as long as I had this man by my side.

He sucked me down and all thought of the future fled. My pleasure at the moment moved to the fore as he ran his teeth up and down my length. His hands held my hips in place. The rough pads of his thumbs made little circles against my inner thigh.

Higher and higher I climbed. I didn't want to come. Truly, I wanted this pleasure to last forever.

Then he speared my slit with his tongue and it was pretty much over. I managed to pant that I was coming as he continued to suck. He had a chance to pull off, but he doubled down and the end for me came hard and fast. I cried out my gratification as the orgasm ripped through me.

Jesus, had it ever felt that good? Like coming apart at the seams and being stitched back together with loving care. He crawled up my body and took my mouth in a passionate kiss. I tasted myself, and that lit another fire in me. These delights—these moments of connection—I wanted them to last forever.

Finally he pulled back. His pupils were blown in the low light and I suspected mine were much the same. "Can I fuck you?"

I considered. "Sure."

He cocked his head.

"I, uh..." I scratched my stubble. "I was hoping you could make love to me. I mean if you want—"

He dove in for another toe-curling kiss. He meandered his hand down my flank and slid it under me so he could cup my ass. Finally he pulled back. He nuzzled my neck as he whispered, "With pleasure." After placing a kiss just below my ear, he peppered my cheek and then jaw with little pecks. He sucked on my neck and then went lower still, taking my nipple into his mouth. I'd never been turned on by this, but it did something to me tonight. His care and exquisite gentleness touched a part of my soul I never bared to anyone.

He drew his hand around my pelvis and grazed my cock.

I'd have sworn nothing was going to happen, but those rough calluses against my tender flesh caused a fire to light in my belly.

He grinned. Then he knelt and snagged a condom, which he rolled on dextrously.

Ah, good, he'd searched the bag. As I hoped he would.

He opened the bottle of lube and squeezed some onto his fingers.

I grasped my knees and pulled them up and out of the way.

After he gazed at me for what felt like forever, he lowered his hand and pressed a finger inside me.

Powerless to do otherwise, I moaned.

He slid his finger in again then added a second.

Heat coursed through my veins.

He scissored, he twisted, and then, as if he'd done it a hundred times before, he hit my prostate.

I gasped.

His grin was infectious and wicked. He tapped me lightly a couple of times before withdrawing his fingers.

I barely had time to miss them before he slathered lube onto his cock and slid into me.

The burn was manageable as he stretched me open, and the relief was welcomed when he pressed the head of his cock in. From there he slid leisurely in and out as he advanced farther and farther inside me. Before I realized it, he'd seated himself.

Our gazes clashed as he sought permission. Permission I'd give him a hundred times over.

He moved.

I shifted.

He withdrew.

I inhaled.

He pushed back inside.

I exhaled.

I needed more, but didn't know how to ask for it. I'd requested he make love to me. And I had no regrets, but I also wanted...force? Passion?

His all-knowing grin warmed me.

He understood. He withdrew almost completely and then pressed home. Then he did it again. And again. Each time he did, he increased the force.

Each thrust pushed me higher and higher—metaphorically and literally.

I banged my head against the headboard and he winced.

Quickly, I secured a pillow behind my head so it wouldn't happen again. "*Please.*" I wasn't above begging. Anything to have him bring me to the edge again. My previously deflated cock was springing back to life, and I was ready for another shot at coming.

As if sensing my need, he grasped my cock and grinned.

"Twenty-four." My pithy comment.

"Yeah, I'm only twenty-eight." His witty comeback.

I couldn't remember if I knew that, but he felt years older. More mature. He'd been working for five years while I languished at the university. A world separated us, and yet, in that moment, the distance felt paltry.

He tugged, and I refocused. This. All I ever wanted, and I was getting it.

He resumed his ministrations as he worked me back into a frenzy.

His jerks of my cock matched the rhythm of his thrusts, and soon, despite my wish to keep going like this forever, I was coming.

The force of the orgasm took me by surprise. As my cum spurted over his hand, some of it landed on my belly.

And still he maintained his rhythm. His neck muscles strained as he thrust over and over again.

Then, quite suddenly, he stilled.

Our gazes locked. In that moment, I saw into his soul. The loneliness. The isolation. The grief over losing his only living relative in this country. A man who hadn't loved him because of who he was. I almost blurted out that I loved him. Or that I could love him. That if he gave me a chance, we could make something of this. A forever because of a storm. A forever based on mutual attraction and more.

I couldn't explain it. It made no sense. Yet all I knew was I never wanted to leave his arms.

Fuck me.

Chapter Eight

Isaac

Holy fuck.

I was a goner.

Hours had passed since our passionate bout of lovemaking, and still sleep eluded me. After I'd come, I withdrew carefully. I knotted off the condom and then went into the bathroom to soak a washcloth in hot water. I brought it back to our bed where I set about gently cleaning Ben.

He bestowed upon me a sleepy, sated smile, and soon slipped into sleep.

Normally after a good orgasm, I was able to drift off as well.

Not tonight.

Tonight I was energized. Or keyed up. Wound up like a top about to explode into action as soon as the string was released. Instead of disrupting my bed partner's sleep with my restlessness, I dressed in my T-shirt and sleep pants. I snagged my laptop and headed over to the couch by the fire.

Within seconds of my butt hitting the cushions, I had company next to me.

Buddy gave me the most beseeching look, and I didn't have the heart to boot him. Plus, this was a pet-friendly room. No way was this adorable beagle the first canine to grace the couch.

He pawed at my forearm and tilted his head.

I met his gaze, then scratched behind his ears.

He sighed.

I lifted my arm, and he settled his snout on my thigh.

Okay, then. Phew. If Buddy didn't like me, being a part of Ben's life would've been complicated.

Oh, hell, who was I kidding? Of course this would be complicated. Several hundred miles and a ferry ride separated us. I opened my laptop and navigated my way to my employer's website. No lighthouses in Mission City, but...

Well, if that wasn't a sign, I didn't know what was. I carefully filled out the application for the job of harbormaster in Mission City. I wasn't guaranteed to get it, but the posting had been up for some time. Might've had to do with the salary. I'd be taking a pay cut, but I'd still make enough to survive on.

If he wants you.

Yes, minor hiccup. What if this was one-sided? What if I was just a fling? Someone to pay the bills until he could go back to Mission City? What if he never wanted to see me again?

Movement out of the corner of my eye caught my attention.

Ben, sleep-rumpled and naked, meandered over with a blanket slung over his shoulders. He plopped down next to Buddy, but shifted the pooch so the little guy pretty much sat in my lap. Then he proceeded to kiss my neck. "I woke, and you weren't there." A bit of petulance laced his voice.

"Couldn't sleep."

His stubble rasped my jaw. "I can think of ways to make you sleep." I chuckled.

He snagged my laptop, and before I could react, he had it on his lap. Buddy stirred when I tried to grab it back.

Okay, not upsetting the pup was more important than his master not seeing the website. Nothing confidential as I was on a public site.

Ben blinked. He turned to stare at me. Then his attention was drawn back to the screen emitting a weird blue light that turned his white skin almost translucent.

I'd observed him at dinner, of course, but now I could look my fill. Powerful jaw, distinctive nose, and hair the colour of mahogany close-cropped at the sides. He was just...adorable.

His nose scrunched. Then he rubbed his forehead. "So, uh, you're going to apply for a job in Mission City?"

I tried to read his tone, but he was being scrupulously neutral. "Well, I applied." I rushed to add, "But that doesn't mean I'll get the job and, you know, even if I do, I don't have to take it, and..."

His eyes were bright but wary. "I thought your ex-boyfriend lived in Mission City. Dickens, right?"

"Yes, he does. It'll be nice to reconnect with him. As a friend. We parted on good terms, and I've only ever wanted him to be happy. I'm not the man who can make him happy, though. And he wasn't the man for me."

"But you think I might be?" Again, no hint of what he was thinking.

"Well..." My brain scrambled. How was I supposed to answer that question? We'd made love once. He'd rocked my world. I wanted to see where we could go, and staying in Tofino wasn't going to give me the answer to that question.

Ben gently closed the laptop and set it on the coffee table. Then he carefully scooped Buddy into his arms and placed him on the doggie bed.

Buddy opened one eye, got the lay of the land, and went right back to sleep.

Oh, the life of a dog.

Without warning, Ben hopped onto my lap and straddled me. He ran his hands along my scalp until they rested at my nape. Then he tugged me in for a kiss.

This wasn't a languid kiss. No, this was passion. This was fury. This was need and desire and electricity.

He kissed me with a ferocity that rivaled my own hunger.

I slid the blanket off his shoulders so I could run my hands up and down his back. I cupped his ass, pressing him against me.

His hard cock nudged my belly while mine reacted to the contact.

Could I take him here? On the couch?

Even as I had the thought, he ended the kiss. He pressed his sweat-slicked forehead to mine. "The answer to your question is yes. Hell-fucking-yes."

Had I asked a question? My addled brain couldn't remember. But I'd always remember this moment. The firelight against his skin. The seductive way he bit his lower lip. The promise of more to come. Yeah, good thing he bought a box of condoms.

I hoped the storm lasted forever.

Chapter Nine

Ben

My first Christmas in Mission City was proving to be memorable. I'd convinced my parents to come visit me Christmas Eve so I could show off my new home. The condo I lived in wasn't notable, but this was my first true home of my own. I'd consulted a financial planner and, if all went according to schedule, I'd have my student loans paid off and a nice down payment in just a few years.

My parents had a lot of equity in their home in Burnaby, but they didn't plan to sell anytime soon. Dad confided I'd inherit something down the line, but cautioned me to plan to make my own way in the world as he and Mom intended to live for a good long while.

I was good with that.

My younger sister opted to go to a movie with friends rather than see my new digs, but we'd never been close. Not for lack of effort on my part. She just thought I was, you know, boring.

Marisa called to wish me well and wailed about the unfairness of being stuck on Vancouver Island for what she claimed would be the rest of her miserable life. Yeah, until she struck out on her own, her parents owned her. Hopefully teaching would bring her some joy.

Mom and Dad nibbled on crackers as I cooked up a feast.

Well, a ham with instructions, some cored pineapple, and cooked asparagus.

Mom enjoyed her wine while Dad gazed out my sliding glass door. "It's a nice view."

My condo looked out over the Fraser Valley and over to the Abbotsford mountains.

That wasn't why I chose it, but I could admit I'd done well. "On a clear day, you can see Mount Baker."

Hopefully it would remain the dormant volcano in Washington State.

"Yes, lovely." Mom took another sip of wine. "Are you certain you don't need my help?"

Only her eighth offer.

"Really, I'm good." I checked the timer. "In fact, why don't you have a seat at the table?"

I'd found the table and chairs at a local charity shop. I intended to put aside every penny I could toward owning my own home. When I bought, then I could spend a bit on nice furniture.

Dad held a chair for Mom.

She offered him a genuine smile when he pushed her chair in and sat himself.

My parents were old-school traditionalists. Thirty years of marriage, two kids, a house in the burbs...everything I aspired to.

I wanted to be just like them.

A knock at the door caught me off-guard. I was curious because I'd need to buzz in any guests. Was this one of my neighbors? Had I already offended someone?

I opened the door and my breath caught.

Isaac stood there.

Breath-stealingly handsome and slightly disheveled. I arched a brow.

"My replacement was late. I raced to catch the bus, raced to catch the ferry, raced to catch the bus, then raced to catch the train—"

I pressed my finger to his lips. "I thought you wouldn't be here until the New Year."

He kissed my finger. "That was the plan, but when I was showing the new guy around, he confessed that his ex-girlfriend booted him and he was couch surfing. I asked if he wanted to start early and, to say he was eager is an understatement." He glanced over my shoulder. "I should've called. Except I wanted to surprise you."

Buddy, who'd been napping on the nice used couch, apparently chose this moment to awaken. He scrambled off the couch and tore across the floor, eventually barreling into Isaac.

My man scooped the excited dog into his arms and allowed himself to be subjected to a barrage of doggie kisses. "Yes, I missed you too."

"Darling, are you going to introduce us to your friend?"

My mother's voice pulled me away from the joyous reunion. I eyed Isaac's one suitcase.

"They're shipping the other suitcase and my two boxes of books." He shrugged. "I travel light."

"You'll never have to travel again," I whispered before grabbing the suitcase and wheeling it inside.

Isaac didn't surrender his doggie shield when he faced my parents, both of whom had risen.

"Mom, Dad, this is Isaac. Isaac, this is Carol and Bob Whitaker."

My father stuck out his hand, but quickly pulled it back when he realized Isaac wasn't going to relinquish my wriggling dog.

Had Isaac ever met *the parents* before? I couldn't remember if he had met Dickens's. Of course, we didn't spend a lot of time talking about our ex-boyfriends. We did spend a lot of time talking about our future.

"Darling, what's that smell?"

Oh shit.

I dropped the suitcase and bolted to the oven. I opened it and a waft of crispy-meat smell washed over me. I glanced over at three people gaping at me. The three most important people of my life.

"I hope you don't mind crispy."

Buddy yipped.

Make that three people and one canine.

After three hours, my parents took their leave. They secured a promise from Isaac that he'd come with me to their house tomorrow for Christmas Day. I swore my mother got teary when he admitted he had no close family in Canada. Oh well, he did now.

Midnight approached as we slid into our new bed. Here, I'd refused to scrimp.

Isaac was going to pay half the rent and agreed saving up for our own place was a good idea.

My head still spun at how quickly things moved. Phone calls and email whenever he was available. Me making a second trip to Tofino and this time sneaking out to see the lighthouse. We might or might not've made love in some interesting places. Given how fucking cold this time of year was...daring came to mind.

"I can't believe you're here."

He opened his arms, and I dove into them.

As he wrapped me in an embrace, I melted. Turned all gooey inside. Reveled in his strength. I pressed my hand to his sternum, running my fingers through his coarse chest hair. "No regrets?"

As he cocked his head, the light from the streetlamps highlighted his features.

We needed to get blackout blinds.

"Regret you? Never." He said the word with vehemence. "Now, let me show you how much I appreciate you."

With that, we made love long into the night.

Epilogue

Isaac

Showing up at The Owl's Nest to let Dickens know I'd moved to Mission City was easier than I expected.

He knew of Ben and seemed genuinely pleased for both of us. Glowing with new love, he promised to introduce me to his new beau.

I was happy for him.

My job as harbormaster differed greatly from lightkeeper. All these people. Less so, given winter was well and truly entrenched. But come summer, the place'd be hopping.

I was locking up for the night on my fifth day on the job when a familiar car turned into the parking lot. The walk home was twenty-minutes uphill, but I didn't mind. Gave me time to settle the day and clear my mind. Yet, Ben had shown up three of the past five days.

"Hop in, it's cold."

Barely at the freezing mark and no wind today. Tofino had high winds and was below freezing.

I might've been keeping track. Just wishing the new guy luck. Here I tracked river levels, debris, and snow packs. The more snow that fell, the higher the river would crest in the spring. Something to monitor.

I slid into Ben's ten-year-old Honda. Somewhere on the list of things to buy was a newer car for him. Then he planned to gift me this one. I didn't need a car, but he pointed out it'd be handy on the days of torrential downpours that were common in the Fraser Valley.

He wasn't wrong.

I leaned over to give him a kiss on his cheek, but at the last moment, he turned, and our lips met. We might've lingered a bit with that one.

He grunted. "Now I want to take you home."

"So take me home."

"But I wanted to take you out to Stavros's tonight."

"We can go another night." Truthfully, I looked forward to a night of quiet and could wait to try the local Greek restaurant everyone raved about.

"I made reservations." A slight tinge of exasperation.

Whether at me or himself, I couldn't tell. "Then by all means, let's go."

It took little time, and soon we parked in the lot behind the restaurant.

I was about to get out of the car when Ben put a restraining hand on my arm. I cocked my head.

"I just..." His blue eyes shone with worry in the streetlight.

Night came early in January.

"We don't have to go." Discomfort settled in my chest. "I mean, if it's important to you, then of course we'll go. I'm sure they'd be okay if we begged off."

"No." He cleared his throat. "We're going." He unbuckled his seatbelt and got out of the car.

I followed suit. What was going on?

We walked up the staircase and stepped inside the warm and welcoming space.

A gigantic man greeted us with a massive smile. "You must be Ben and Isaac. Everyone is here."

Everyone?

Hell, I hardly knew anyone.

Ben snagged my hand and led me to the back of the restaurant.

His parents were there. His sister Carson sat next to them, looking utterly bored. Dickens and his man Spike were also here.

Before I had a chance to react, Ben dropped to one knee.

Carson snickered, their mom gasped, their dad chuckled, and Dickens and Spike gaped.

So did I.

Ben held out a ring. "I know what you're going to say."

That was rather presumptuous of him, seeing as I had no idea what to say.

"Or I think I know," he corrected. "That we've only known each other for six weeks. That it's too soon. That, uh, we've only been living together for two weeks. And that, you know, we need time to get to know each other."

All that was absolutely true, yet one other thing was also true.

I loved him.

With my whole heart and my whole soul. He was the person I'd searched for all these years, but didn't believe I'd ever find.

I got down on one knee as well and met his gaze. "I love you, Ben. And I'm not just saying that because you're offering me a ring—although that'd be a great reason. No, from the first night we met, I knew. As we sat in the restaurant in Tofino, with Buddy at our feet, I had a sense of coming home. You offered me sanctuary during a storm—now I offer you my heart." I grasped his cheeks and pulled him in for a kiss. A kiss I poured all my love into. A kiss I wanted to last forever.

"Can we eat now? I'm hungry."

Good God, Carson whined like a two-year-old, not a woman of twenty.

Yet Ben grinned, undaunted by his sister's rudeness. He slipped the ring onto my finger.

A little loose, but we could get that taken care of. We rose, a little unsteadily, and took our seats at the table.

Within moments, the large man—who I assumed was Stavros—appeared with a bottle of champagne. He popped the cork and filled everyone's glasses.

As he did, I leaned over to whisper into Ben's ear. "What if I said no?"

He met my gaze. "Then I would've spent the next twenty years convincing you." He pressed a hand to my cheek. "We can wait as long as you want. I just...needed you to know how I felt."

I glanced around the table. "Well, no worries on that score." I pressed a kiss to his lips. This one, given our company, was chaste. "You realize I'm a forever kind of guy."

"We're going to have a forever love affair."

And we did.

Enjoyed Ben and Isaac's story? There's more Mission City! Flip the page for a low-angst second chance romance...

Marcus's Cadence

A Mission City gay romance short story

Gabbi Grey

*W*hat happens when your biggest crush turns up on your doorstep after twelve years?

Cadence Crawford has a good thing going. He's making waves as a realtor in Mission City, British Columbia. Yes, he's recently suffered a personal loss, but he's moving on, and his path forward includes selling the only true home he's ever known.

Marcus Brannigan is doing fine. He has his physiotherapy practice, he watches over his younger twin sisters, and he's happy. When he unexpectedly runs into Cadence, who is selling the home he's always coveted, he's prepared to do some negotiating.

Neither knew they were seriously crushing on each other. Now they've admitted the truth, is happily ever after in the cards?

Marcus's Cadence is a 7k second-chance gay romance instalove short story with a very happy ending and a malti-poo named Kiki.

Contents

Chapter One

Cadence

Oh shit, oh shit, oh shit.

The words ricocheted around in my brain. Shannon Branigan's older brother was here. In person. Right here. In—

"Can I come in?"

Uh...

Stay calm.

Marcus had to be here to see the property, because he sure as shit wasn't here for me. "Of course." I held the door and carefully gauged his body language as he stepped in. Nice tight ass in formfitting jeans—

"Why is the place for sale? I mean, these cottages are never available."

Pain shot through me like a knife, visceral and white-hot.

Deep breath.

"Miss Mabel died a while back, and Gertie decided to move to Arizona with her grandkids." My attempt at hiding my misery failed, judging by the pity on Marcus' face. "They were the lesbian couple who took me in after my bigoted parents turfed me."

His brow furrowed. "I...when? I mean, how old were you?"

Acid churned my gut. "Fifteen."

"Shit...I mean, you and Shan were dance partners back then. How did I not know?"

Because you and your hockey jock friends didn't pay any attention to little gay dancers like me?

"I didn't tell a lot of people back then." Or now.

"But Shan knew." Certainty. As solidly spoken as the man himself. All six-foot-two, dark-brown hair and eyes, muscled physique... *Don't go there.* "Look, Marcus, that happened a long time ago, before Shan's accident, before—"

With a step, he invaded my personal space. "You should've told me. I would've..."

"What? Taken care of me? Given me a home? Miss Mabel and Gertie did. I was fine. I *am* fine." Lonely, but fine.

"Oh, you're fine, alright."

I cocked my head.

He shrugged. Then he spun and tapped the wall. "Want to give me a tour?"

Right up to my bedroom? Sure.

Or not.

"Just on the market and a good price." I handed him the brochure and his brows shot up. Although Gertie would enjoy the extra money to spoil her grandkids, she didn't need it. She was splitting part of the profits with me, but I was more concerned about finding the right buyer. "I'm hoping whomever buys it won't tear it down."

His eyes widened in evident horror. "This house is practically on the heritage list. It'd be a travesty to tear it down."

Well, hadn't quite achieved official heritage status, but it meant a lot to me. So did his obvious horror at destroying the one place I felt truly safe.

"Why are you selling it?"

The question startled me. "Well, with Gertie gone, it seemed silly to hold on to it. I have my condo…" And why wasn't I just moving back in? I could sell the condo and send the money to Gertie. Hell, she'd gift me the house if she knew I was staying in it. I thought part of her heart was breaking selling the thing. She was as adamant as me about not tearing the grand dame down. But I couldn't control what a buyer chose to do. I could only choose a buyer carefully.

We wandered into the kitchen. "All the appliances are updated. We did the wiring back in the late nineties when technology took a huge leap forward. The ladies had all the most modern amenities."

Marcus spun in the space. "Yet kept all its charm. I love the yellow paint. So bright."

I'd once thought it dated. Now, in his eyes, the appeal was clear. I pointed to the huge windows. "With the southern exposure, this room is really bright on a sunny day."

Uh, why was he staring at me like that? I forced myself to not turn around to see if there was something interesting behind me.

"The laundry room is in the basement. Bit of a hassle, but typical for these old places. There's a recreation room downstairs that could be converted into an exercise room. And it's accessible from the side of the house. No stairs. You could install a bathroom down there."

And still his eyes ate me up.

"There are three bedrooms upstairs. The master isn't a bad size. My bedroom is decent as well, and the third is currently a sewing room. But you could turn that into a small office."

"Your boyfriend not want to move in?"

"My...?" I furrowed my brow.

"You were with that guy." He gesticulated in some undiscernible manner.

"Oh, yeah, that guy." I knew who he was referring to. Or at least I thought he did. "We didn't last long. I was into monogamy. He apparently wasn't." I hadn't been all that upset when I booted the asshole to the curb. Better to take out the trash before it stank up my pristine house.

"And you're not with anyone?"

Where is he going with this? He advanced toward me. I backed up a step.

He halted.

But I didn't want him to.

He opened his arms and I stepped into the embrace. A hug, right? I bit my lip.

He licked his. "I want to kiss you."

That was all the warning I got. I could've said no. Could've held up my hand. He'd stop.

He sucked on my lower lip, coaxing my mouth open.

Oh... The thrust of tongue matched the grinding of hips and, *holy hell*, my cock hardened. When it brushed Marcus's erection, life suddenly looked very different.

Yanking my mouth away, I fought for breath. "You're gay?" Dumbest question ever, right? But he'd never even hinted at being gay, while I'd flaunted it. Gertie and Miss Mabel had told me to rejoice in being unique and beautiful. They loved me the way I was.

"I've always wanted you—always loved you."

"But you never said..."

"Sweetheart, you were underage." He pressed a kiss to my temple and sucked on my earlobe. "Tell me I'm not too late. I want this house...and goddamn, I want you." He ground our pelvises together. Cock to fucking cock. "Need you."

"Let me take down the *Open House* sign."

"And if someone else shows up?"

"They're fucked."

"Oh, someone is definitely getting fucked. And I hope it's me."

OMG. Marcus Branigan wanted me—little Cadence Crawford, was going to buy the cottage, *and* was a bottom? Fuck, life had never looked brighter. "Let me show you to my room."

"*Our* room."

Oh, fuck, yes.

Chapter Two

Marcus

When I saw the sign for the Open House, I nearly drove off the road in my haste to pull a U-turn and get here as fast as I could. I'd wanted one of these cottages for as long as I remembered. Had prized the things. Coveted them.

Dreamed to make one mine.

Did I expect Cadence Crawford to answer the door?

Hell no.

Was I thrilled?

Fuck yes.

Somewhere, in the recesses of my mind, I remembered hearing he was a realtor. The kid, make that, gorgeous man had always been ambitious, and that industry certainly demanded cutthroat tactics.

I followed him back through the house and waited impatiently as he went outside to retrieve the sign. At least the house was mine. I could afford the price. It'd be tight, but I'd make it work.

He gave me a wicked grin as he grasped my hand and led us up the rickety staircase, I admired both his ass and the fine construction of the house. It had to be seventy or eighty years old, but she had good bones. I envisioned my living space on the ground floor, with an accessible bedroom for Shannon, as well as a couple of bedrooms up here. If they were small, I might knock out a wall and create one massive room. And likely the bathroom would need upgrading. Dollar signs clouded my vision.

"I'll show you the master first."

He had said *our* room. Had he moved into Gertie and Mabel's bedroom? I followed him into the space and the explosion of floral décor nearly floored me.

Shannon, a girly girl, hasn't had these many flowers.

The bedspread, the drapes, the wallpaper, the dust ruffle...the stuff was everywhere.

"You didn't redecorate?"

His casual shrug didn't fool me.

"I figured the next owners would do that."

"You couldn't bear it, could you?"

Piercing blue eyes lit with an intensity I rarely witnessed.

"No, I couldn't. Miss Mabel loved floral. Gertie didn't want it in the rest of the house, but she acquiesced here." He ran his hand across the bedspread. "I know it won't stay this way. Nor should it. But I couldn't be the one to do it. Might I make a few less bucks? Sure. But my heart stays intact."

God, he was killing me. I touched his arm, and he leaned into it. "She had a good life. And Gertie's not gone yet."

"It still hurts."

"Yeah, it does." He pressed his hand to mine and we held still. Then he shook his head. "Bathroom."

There was only one on this floor, and although an ensuite would be nice, I was willing to make any kind of accommodations to get this place. I poked my head in, looked around, then pulled back. "The seventies called, they want their paisley back."

He guffawed. "That was the last time the place was renovated." He tapped the wall. "You could do a total gut job or just a remodel."

Those dollar signs were getting bigger every moment.

"Let's see the sewing room."

He pointed to an open door.

I stepped into the room. The sloped ceiling meant I had to duck.

A bench seat sat in front of the dormer window which looked out over the street.

"Miss Mabel sat and sewed there well into her nineties. She only gave it up when her vision failed her."

I glanced over to him as he smiled.

"And yes, at least it's dusky rose and not Pepto-Bismol pink."

The room needed a paint job, and I wasn't convinced it'd stay the same color. "This would make a great kid's bedroom."

He met my gaze. "If one is inclined to have children. Yes, this room and mine are perfect for kids."

"You were going to show me your bedroom?" I wanted to ask him how he felt about children, but the moment felt too tenuous. We were too early into this.

Whatever this was.

I followed him out of the room. We passed the open door to the linen closet and then were at the last door.

"In here." Cadence's cheeks pinkened as I passed him.

His blue eyes sparkled, as they always did when he was amused. His hair was longer than he used to keep it, almost to his shoulders, and the dark waves curled in that perfect way I loved. I wanted to hold on and never let go. His cheekbones were sharper than when he was younger. More sculpted. And that dimple on his chin got me every time.

Focus.

I pivoted. The space was roomier than I expected. The dark-wood paneling was very retro. A desk sat in front of a window looking south. I headed that way. The view, despite the pouring rain, was amazing—the southern part of Mission City, the bridge to Abbotsford, and the mountains beyond. "I bet you can see Baker on a sunny day."

"You can." The smile lit his voice. "I spent a lot of time daydreaming while watching the dormant volcano."

I turned back. "What did you dream of?"

"Fame. Fortune. Being the best ballet dancer in the world." He ducked his head for a moment before looking back and meeting my gaze. "You."

Why did that word make me sad and happy at the same time? Sad for the time we lost and happy because we'd found each other again. I eyed the double bed. Our fit would be tight. "You want to talk?" That was the right thing to do. I mean, we hadn't spent five minutes in each other's company in about twelve years. Cadence came by a few times after Shan's accident. But she sent him away—as she had everyone else—and he hadn't had a reason to come back. I didn't blame him. But I'd missed him. His quirky sense of humor. His lovely laugh. His smile that went on forever.

"Can we talk later?" He bit his lower lip. "You said I could fuck you, and given how many times I fantasized about just that, I really want action now and talk later."

My cock leapt back to life. I could do this. I might be a little out of practice, but I could do this. "How do you want me?"

"On your back. I want to look you in the eyes when you come."

Well, that was good enough for me.

Chapter Three

Cadence

I hoped he'd just shed his clothes quickly and hop on the bed, but no such luck.

He removed his coat and hung it over the back of the desk chair. He toed off the shoes he probably should've removed when he came into the house.

I'd been so stunned that practicalities like that escaped me.

He unbuttoned his flannel shirt leisurely, revealing rippling muscles.

I didn't think he played hockey anymore, but as a physiotherapist, he'd need to stay in shape. Each time I drove past his clinic, my heart stuttered. I'd heard somewhere he was living in a condo in downtown Mission City, but I hadn't known which one.

His hands moved to his belt buckle, and I salivated. *Yes, big boy, show me all you've got.*

Each time I drove past his family's home—where his twin sisters still lived—my heart ached. Twelve years was a long time. Too much water under the bridge at this point. Not that I didn't think of my former dance partner often and, okay, so not the time to be thinking of Marcus's sister.

He opened the belt, unbuttoned his fly, and slid down the zipper. Gray boxer briefs.

Yeah, that fit his personality.

He tucked his thumbs in both underwear and jeans and slid them down in one fluid movement. He shucked them and hung them over the chair as well, then he turned to me.

That wicked grin hit me low in the gut. Naked, he was a thing of beauty. All sinew and muscle, and skin pale in the weak winter light. In the summer, though, it often went a light brown when he spent time out in the sun. Beach volleyball and running, if memory served.

And it did. I remembered. I remembered everything.

His cock jutted out, and he grasped it. "Are you going to join me, or is this a solo show?"

Again, I licked my lips. "Oh, this is a duet." I yanked down the comforter and top sheet. "Lie down."

He winked and did just that, settling in the center of the bed.

At lightning speed, I shed my own clothes. I tossed them haphazardly over the desk chair, never letting my gaze wander from his. His eyes were almost black in this light. Slitted, and eating me up. Devouring me with his gaze.

By the time I removed my dress socks, my cock was leaking pre-cum. I palmed myself, willing my raging hard-on to wait one fucking minute.

His gaze moved from mine to my cock, and then back up. "Please tell me you have lube and condoms."

Right.

Had almost forgotten. I yanked open the nightstand drawer and stuck my hand into the very back. I'd refreshed the stash a couple of years ago because I often spent the night here and occasionally had company. If Gertie knew, she never said. She and Mabel honestly didn't care, as long as I was safe. They taught me about condoms when they were in their late eighties. A lesson I'd likely never forget. I could be one hundred like Miss Mabel had been and would still flush as the two women sat me down for *the talk*. Still made me smile.

"You coming over here, or are you going to bask in that memory?"

"A good one, I promise." I dropped the lube and a strip of condoms on the bed. "You up for this, old man?"

His affronted look was adorable.

"I'm thirty-one." He sucked in his abs. "I have a while to go before I'm an old man."

Fair enough.

I knelt on the bed and crawled atop him. I let my weight settle as he opened his legs and let me lay between his thighs. His skin was warm as I traced his cheekbones. His stubble was barely there. Had he shaved today? Had he worked today? I hadn't asked how he wound up in my neck of the woods, but it didn't matter. He was here now, and I planned to take full advantage.

Telegraphing the kiss, I moved slowly. Deliberately. He ran his hands through my hair and tugged lightly. Pulled me closer to him.

Our lips met, and he immediately opened for me.

I took full advantage, thrusting my tongue in. I wanted to claim him. Own him. Mark him as mine. Ruin him for any other man.

Wait...what?

This was just a fling, right? I mean, not even a fling. Just a fuck. Because there couldn't be anything more between us.

Why not?

Before I could wage the internal debate, Marcus slid his hand down my side to my flank, then across to my ass. He grasped a cheek, squeezed it, then thrust up against me. Our cocks brushed. My insides lit.

I broke the kiss and pulled away, then shimmied down his body until I was between his thighs.

His cock angled up toward his stomach—red, angry, and leaking precum.

I swiped my tongue across the head.

He bucked.

A grin spread across my face. I grasped his cock and gave it a good couple pumps.

"Jesus, Cadence."

The way he said my name—through gritted teeth—made me smile.

Our gazes locked, and I gauged every nuance of pleasure I could wring from him as I licked his cock from root to tip. I sucked on the head and flicked the slit with my tongue.

His eyes rolled back.

Swallowing him down was easy. Holding myself in check as I fucked him with my mouth was a whole other thing. Our gazes locked again, and his pupils blew wide as I edged him closer to orgasm.

Whimpers and moans and sighs escaped him. He grasped the sheet and tugged.

I sucked harder.

"Please, stop." A hoarse whisper.

Immediately, I pulled back.

"No," he howled.

I cocked an eyebrow.

He winced. "I was coming."

"So...what's your point?"

"I was going to come in your mouth." His brow furrowed.

"I wanted you to come in my mouth." This wasn't supposed to be complicated.

"I, uh, you like that?"

He seemed genuinely confused.

"I love that. Why, don't you?"

That brow knit further.

Oh, shit.

"Have you done this before?" I tried to ask lightly, but the weight of it filled the room.

He shut his eyes. His cheeks reddened.

I needed clarification. "You said you wanted me to fuck you—"

"—and I do—"

"But have you ever done that before?"

Silence.

Finally, his eyes opened. "Have I done stuff to myself? Yes. Have I been with another man? No."

"Are you out?" I hadn't heard anything either way, but this was truly none of my business. Except I needed to know. His head was somewhere, and I wasn't convinced it was here.

"I was going to. I swear. When I finished undergrad and got into med school, I planned to tell my parents and sister. But then, you know, stuff happened."

"Shannon's accident."

He nodded. "And I didn't get into medical school, and suddenly it didn't feel like the right time. So I studied to be a physiotherapist and have lived my life."

"Alone."

He nodded.

"Celibate." Not to put too fine a point to it.

He nodded.

"Not even a woman? Have you dated?"

This time, he shook his head.

"And no one noticed?" I was perversely curious. His family had always been tight. I'd envied that. Especially after my own summarily booted me out.

"Zach and West noticed my lack of dating at the university, but we haven't seen each other since the crash. I think Casey's noticed, but she's never said anything."

Casey, Shannon's twin, was his other younger sister.

"So basically, you're a virgin." He'd been so aggressive downstairs, I never thought to question it.

If possible, his cheeks went even redder.

"Yeah. Basically."

Oh, this was going to be so much fun.

Chapter Four

Marcus

Oh. My. God.

Why? Why had I been so honest? I could've pulled it off. He'd never have known.

You think so?

No, he would've known. This was Cadence. He knew everything.

Well, not *everything*.

He hadn't known I was gay. Or that I'd crushed on him since we were teenagers. But he'd been Shannon's dance partner. He'd been like a little brother to me. So, yeah, not cool. I headed to university with plans to come out after graduating. Life intervened, and that never happened. What did that make me? A thirty-one-year-old virgin.

Not a complete virgin. I had toys. Did that count?

Probably not.

Cadence sucked my cock down his throat again.

Jesus.

I kept saying that. Part prayer, part worship. I mean, I always assumed a blow job would feel amazing. But Cadence blowing me? Better than any dream I could ever come up with. His mouth was warm, wet, and inviting. He held my hips in place, preventing me from bucking up. "I really am coming."

He sucked harder.

I gave up the battle.

The orgasm tore through me, ripping my sanity from me. Electricity arced through me. It singed my hair, curled my toes, and fried the circuits in my brain.

And still Cadence sucked.

Jesus, there wasn't going to be anything of me left by the time he finished.

I was completely okay with that.

Pressing the heel of my hand to my forehead, I let out a jagged exhalation. I jolted when Cadence pulled off with a pop. He pressed a kiss to my flaccid dick, then he crawled back up my body and, before I had a moment to think, he thrust his tongue in my mouth. I'd tasted my cum before, but this was different. Hotter. More carnal. Sexier.

He pulled back with a wicked grin on his face. "Do you trust me?"

"Of course." And I did. Implicitly. With my whole soul.

"Great, spread your legs."

I did. He rocked back on his heels, so he sat between my thighs. He stroked my sensitive cock once before palming my balls and rolling them in his hand.

More sensation ricocheted through me. I couldn't even identify all the feelings his tenderness evoked in me. I moaned when he released me but perked right up when he snagged the lube.

"I need to get you warmed up."

I was already pretty warm.

He pressed a finger to my entrance.

Oh. Okay, yep, kind of cold. And unexpected, although not unpleasant.

He pressed a hand to my sternum. "Breathe with me, Marcus."

I liked the way he said my name. Light. Breathy. I did as instructed.

After a few breaths, he pressed his finger in.

I met his gaze, then gave a slight nod.

He increased to two fingers.

The burn wasn't overwhelming, but it held me captive in the moment. He twisted and scissored, then he crooked his finger and holy hell, he hit my prostate. This wasn't new to me, but the novelty of someone else causing this sensation? Another arc of electricity shot through me.

I moaned.

He grinned. "I want inside you so bad."

"Then do it. Less talk, Cadence, more action."

"But I'm enjoying myself."

I was as well. My cock was certainly perking up and taking notice. Refractory periods were a thing, but maybe I wasn't so far off going again soon.

He withdrew his fingers.

I groaned at the full sensation disappearing. Within moments, though, my belly was aflutter.

He snagged one condom and ripped open the packaging.

I watched with fascination as he rolled the condom onto his length. He'd been so busy pleasuring me that I hadn't been paying attention. I was now. He was slender and long. Longer than me.

"Bring your knees up to your chest. Up and out." His grin was wicked. "I want to see all of you."

I paused. What if he didn't like what he saw? What if I was a disappointment? I'd never put myself on full display like this.

He rubbed my thighs as he gently coaxed me to follow his instructions.

After another moment, I realized it didn't matter.

He didn't care what I looked like. He cared about who I was on the inside.

He always had, and I was pretty sure he always would. I grasped my knees and pulled them up.

He slathered lube onto his cock.

My insides turned to liquid. My blood heated. My body tensed with anticipation.

He eased a finger inside me. "You're going to be okay. I'll take care of you."

And he would. I tried to open for him. To let him know I was ready. For anything.

He crooked his finger and hit my prostate again.

Pleasure again zipped through my body.

Then his finger slipped away, and his cock slowly replaced it. He probed my entrance and held my gaze as he slid in, millimeter by millimeter.

At first, everything felt good. My confidence grew.

Not so bad.

Until he pressed his entire head inside.

The burn intensified.

"Breathe."

I couldn't. The breath was being stolen from me. I felt like I was ripping in two.

He began to withdraw.

"No." Through gritted teeth. I could do this. I wanted to do this. Hell, I *needed* to do this. Yes, I'd eventually forgive myself for tapping out, but I didn't want that to be my memory of the first time. I could survive this—as long as Cadence was with me.

Bearing down, I breathed through the pain. His blue eyes held me mesmerized. He gave a perceptible nod, and I nodded back.

Again, back to the incremental easing into me.

As the burn receded, a sense of well-being settled. I often counseled clients that sometimes pain was a good thing. And to others, it was the body's signal to stop. Today, as pain ebbed into something less tangible, I knew the former was true. Yes, intellectually I wanted this. But, in my heart, my body wanted it too. To feel connected to someone. To touch and be touched. To have a bond so missing in my everyday life.

Cadence stroked my cheek, brushing away the errant tear. "This is killing me. Hurting you like this."

"It doesn't hurt as much. It, uh, feels…" I struggled for the right word. Not good, but not bad. "Please keep going. I'll die if you stop now." Better to get this done. Maybe not the most logical sentiment, but I knew myself.

"You're so brave. I think that's what I love most about you. Despite everything, you kept going. That's true bravery."

What he loved *most* about me? No, wait, what he *loved* about me.

Did that mean he loved me?

Too much thinking.

I closed my eyes, trying to ward off the pain.

"Open your eyes, baby. I need to see you. I need to know you're okay."

And I was. Okay. I was more than okay. I opened my eyes and saw nothing but compassion.

"I'm all the way in." He feathered my hair and stroked his knuckles against my stubbled cheek. "Are you sure?"

"Never more sure. About anything." I needed to convince him. Let him see the earnestness of the moment. The voracity of my will.

"Okay." He pulled back.

I did my best not to wince.

He arched an eyebrow.

A perfect eyebrow. God, everything about him was perfect. "Again, please." I wasn't above begging.

He pressed back in.

I arched to meet him.

He withdrew and pressed back in again.

I held his gaze.

"Normally I would tell you to jack yourself, but you might be sore—"

I grasped my cock. I wasn't sore. And given my dick was half-hard and dying for attention, this seemed like a logical plan. I tugged experimentally. I got harder.

Yeah, and the pain in my ass receded farther. He continued to move in and out of me slowly, and the pain took a back seat to the pleasure.

Precum leaked from my tip, and I smeared it down my length. Not enough to eliminate the friction, but enough to distract me from other things going on.

"God, baby, you're so tight." Cadence bit his lip.

Both the words and the endearment washed over me in all the good ways. A tension coiled within me. I feeling I recognized well. And yet it felt alien at the same time. "I'm, uh, coming."

"Please do."

Such simple words. Such complicated permission.

Or maybe an easy command to obey. I arched my neck back as I strained against the orgasm. I could do this. All I had to do was let go. Let the pleasure sing through my veins. And as I spurted over my hand, relief flooded my soul.

"Oh, thank Christ." Cadence pushed into me, hard, but it didn't hurt. In turn, he arched his head back, exposing his throat.

With my left hand, I grazed his Adam's apple. I traced down his collarbone, across his chest, and placed my hand over his hammering heart.

He roared his release.

I grinned. Such a loud sound from such a normally delicate person.

He angled his head back so our gazes locked.

I eased my legs back to the mattress as he withdrew.

He crawled up my body and took my mouth.

I gave in to him.

Forever. I wanted this to go on forever.

Chapter Five

Cadence

Words escaped me.

They had to be in there somewhere.

But as Marcus held me in his muscular arms against his broad chest, no truly coherent thoughts could form.

He snagged the comforter and dragged it over us. The fabric was chilled, but it'd warm soon enough from our combined body heat. His cum was also cooling against my stomach, and I needed to remove the condom, but I just couldn't bring myself to give a shit.

As my heart rate returned to normal, I pressed a kiss to his left nipple, right above his heart.

He groaned. "I don't think I have another one in me."

I grinned. "Oh, we're done for the night."

"Really?"

He sounded disappointed. "You want more?" I angled my head so my chin pressed his sternum and our gazes locked. His dark-brown eyes mesmerized. He was so unlike the twins with their blonde hair and their father's silver eyes. Those silver eyes were distinctive and memorable.

Marcus very much favored his mother. Except in height.

Susan Brannigan was definitely on the short side. Yet all the children were tall. The girls were just under six feet and Marcus was over.

When they were young, the girls had been fashion models. Plenty of cute-twins work. Casey'd outgrown that phase, but Shannon had held tight to anything putting her firmly in the spotlight. Dancing, modeling...and she'd planned to add acting to her resumé.

The accident didn't just rob her of her ability to walk. It demolished her ambition. I tried to tell her she could get work, even in a wheelchair, but that'd been twelve years ago when inclusion hadn't really been a thing. Things were different now. Not easy, but views were evolving.

"How are the twins?"

He cocked his head.

"Shan shut me out twelve years ago." Even today, that still stung. Over the past dozen years, I tried a dozen different ways to contact her. Casey barred my entry at the door. Letters were returned unopened. She wasn't on social media.

He feathered a hand through my hair. "She's been through a lot. We all have, but her most of all. And I don't just mean the wheelchair." He closed his eyes for a moment. "Macy's death hit her hard. The four of them were close, but...I don't know..." He appeared to flounder. "Something happened that night. Aside from the accident. I've never been able to get anyone to talk about it."

"Maybe they will. When the time is right."

He tisked. "The time is never right. My parents have moved up to the interior and come home periodically, but it's not the same. They thought leaving Casey, Shan, and Jae together in that house would force them to mature. To go outside of themselves. Never happened. Shan never leaves the house, Casey barely tolerates the outside world, and Jae..." He sighed. "More pain that I can't share."

I wanted to know, but I wouldn't push.

"Maybe, if I try to bring you around, then things will be different."

"As your boyfriend?"

His eyes widened.

Whether in horror or shock, I wasn't sure. Quickly, I pressed my finger to his lips. "It's okay—"

He shook his head, dislodging my finger. "It's not okay. It is so far from okay. I love you. I've always loved you. And you're here, and maybe this is a one-night stand, and maybe we'll never see each other again, and—"

I pressed my finger to his lips. Firmer this time. "This is so the opposite of a one-night stand. It's been a very long time since I've had a man in my bedroom." I winced. "Well, in *this* bedroom." I'd been with a fling just a few weeks ago. It'd ended amicably as we hadn't been interested in being a significant other during the holidays. I'd thought to ring him after the new year. Yep, not gonna happen. "I think Miss Mabel and Gertie would approve. They knew how I felt about you."

He nipped my finger. "You never said."

"We were young. I was Shan's dance partner. You were, as far as I knew, very straight. Very jock. Very macho. I couldn't see you wanting a guy like me."

"Beautiful, lithe, graceful, and with a heart of gold?" He rolled his eyes. "No, I'd never want that."

Fair point.

"But I don't know what to do now."

I cocked my head.

"I'm not ready to come out, but I'm not ready to lose you either."

I pulled him in for a deep kiss. Our tongues parried. My body awoke. I'd never tire of this man.

"You don't have to come out."

"That's not fair to you."

I shook my head. "The right time will come. I believe it in my heart. And if we rekindle our friendship, there's nothing wrong with that. I'm your realtor. Maybe I'll feign a knee injury and you'll have to be my physiotherapist."

He poked my arm. "Don't you dare." He gave me a long penetrating look. "You're really okay with this."

"I am." And I was. I was secure enough with myself that I didn't need external validation. I didn't need everyone to know my business. I'd once been demanding for the spotlight, but those days were long past. These days, I just wanted to be with the man I loved. "I love you. I think I always have, and I know I always will."

He swallowed audibly. "Same for me. That I love you. That I have since we were teenagers. I'm so fucking glad my first time was with you."

"I plan to be your only."

"Yeah, that works. That definitely works."

Before I sat up, he caught sight of the snow globe with a little reindeer that I kept on my nightside table. The one Miss Mabel and Gertie gave me the first Christmas I lived here.

"What are you doing for Christmas?"

Aw, crap. "I, uh, am planning a Harry Potter marathon. With *Die Hard* thrown in for good measure."

He didn't look impressed.

"Marcus, I'll be okay." My first Christmas without Gertie, but I'd manage. We'd do a long video chat.

"I, uh, want you to come with me somewhere."

My ears perked.

"I was planning to go to the animal shelter tomorrow. I've picked out a dog. Today they're cleaning her teeth, and tomorrow she's mine. I mean, if you don't like dogs, I'll understand..."

"Oh my God, I love dogs. How do you not know this about me? And you're adopting a stray? For Christmas?" I lunged up to give him a kiss and our noses collided.

He grunted.

I giggled.

"Whenever she's not with you, I want her with me. It is a she, right?"

"Yeah, Kiki. She's a malti-poo. Her owners abandoned her when they left town. She's about six. Aside from the horrible teeth, she's in good shape."

"Oh, wow, we're like, already having children."

I expected him to balk, but he got a wistful expression. Ah, so kids were on the table. Good to know.

He smiled. "After I spend the day with my family, can I come over? For, you know, Bruce Willis?"

"I happen to have a spare key." I waggled my eyebrows. "And by then you'll be recovered, and we can do this again."

His cheeks went a deep scarlet.

Adorable. I pulled in my stomach, and the skin stuck. "Now, a shower, and then I need sustenance. I'm thinking pizza or Chinese."

"We could head to Fifties and grab burgers."

"You want to be seen in public with me?"

"Yes." He nodded solemnly. "We're buddies hanging out. And, I promise, one day we'll come out as a couple. Just..." Another swallow. "The women are going through something right now, and the timing couldn't be worse."

"I'll wait. For you, I'll wait forever."

"Not forever." His beautiful brow furrowed. "I won't have you thinking you're my dirty secret."

"Well, if we don't have a shower, I will continue to be dirty."

Before I could lever myself away, he pulled me in for another toe-curling kiss.

"Forever," he whispered.

"Forever," I responded.

I planned to hold him to that pledge.

Did you enjoy Marcus and Cadence's story? There are more stories! Turn the page for another scorching short tale.

Not in it for the Money

A Mission City Gay Romance Short Story

GABBI GREY

J ulian

I'm just hanging out on a Friday night, and my boss drops by for comforting. He's mourning his tragic loss, and I'm happy to offer a shoulder to lean on. When the man I've been crushing on for years wants to move things to my bedroom, how can I say no?

August

After the devastating loss of my sister, I turn to the one man who I know will be there for me. I've been in love with my employee for years. Now, as I face the greatest loss of my life, can I find the courage to be my authentic self?

Not in it for the Money is a 5k scorching short story about a boss, his employee, and the inheritance of a lifetime.

Dedication

Randall

Kaje

Contents

Chapter One

Julian

August looked like shit.

He hadn't looked great all week—who would after losing a beloved sister—but today he looked truly awful. And him being in my house spoke volumes. We didn't have *that* kind of relationship. He was my boss. I was his employee. Occasionally, he took us out for a round of drinks. But showing up out of the blue was definitely not him.

My stomach churned as I led him into my living room. Surreptitiously, I sniffed my pits. Showering after work was a necessity, but I always worried the smell of sweat might linger.

The day had been brutally hot. September in southern British Columbia wasn't known for heat, but summer was lingering extra long this year.

Frankly, I wanted the sun to take a break. But that would mean the return of winter, which was equally shitty.

Get over it already.

"You want a drink?" I pointed to my beer.

He dropped onto my couch.

Weary.

That's the word I'd choose. Like he carried the weight of the world on his shoulders.

And maybe he did. Losing Nia had to hurt. She might've been a decade older than him, but at just forty-two, her death felt wrong in so many ways. An aneurysm. And she lived alone. Heck, the coroner said she'd been dead three days before August checked.

That guilt hung like an anvil around his neck. That he couldn't have done anything didn't matter—he felt like he'd let his sister down.

"I don't..." He gazed up at me. His dark-brown eyes begged me to understand. To decide.

I scratched my beard. I couldn't do it. He never drank when he took us out. Once, to me alone, he'd made a comment about an alcoholic mother and an absent father. Hell, Nia had practically raised him from the time he'd been a toddler—taking on the role of mother when she wasn't even a teenager herself.

"Buddy, I don't know how to help you." My chest felt too tight. As it had all week as I watched him suffer. He'd come out to supervise us a few times—we didn't need it, but it made him feel good to be doing something. "Hey, didn't you see Everett today?"

"I don't want to talk about that."

Well, couldn't blame him.

Today'd been the reading of Nia's will.

Everett and August were university buddies—August in forestry management and Everett in pre-law. Their paths had diverged for a while, but both had wound up coming home to Mission City. Now August was an arborist, and Everett was making a name for himself as a lawyer.

I strode to the kitchen. If he wasn't a drinker, I wasn't going to give him booze. If he explicitly asked, I'd consider it. Instead, I yanked a bottle of diet cola from my fridge. I popped the top and took it back to the living room.

August'd pulled one of my throw pillows onto his lap and was hugging it as if it was a lifeline.

Hell, maybe it was.

After putting the cola on the side table by his hand, I dropped onto the couch next to him.

"I can't believe she's gone."

Neither could I.

Their parents passed some time ago. Now, my boss—my friend—was alone in the world.

Given my huge boisterous family and my hearty, healthy parents, I couldn't relate.

Taking him in my arms to drive away some of the pain didn't seem like a good idea, but I needed to form a connection. Slowly, with great care, I eased one of his hands from his death grip on my pillow. I laced our fingers, marveling at the contrast—his so dark and mine so fair.

Although I worked outside, I stayed pale. My grandmother'd had skin cancer when I was in my impressionable early twenties. She made me swear I'd wear sunscreen every day—especially when it became apparent I'd taken to the entire tree-trimming thing that horrified my family.

They wanted a successful professional.

I wanted to be out in nature.

August and I had that in common. Of course, being Black, he didn't get much darker in the summer. But he allowed me to stick a hat on his head on the really sunny days.

"I'm sorry." He turned his head and met my gaze.

Oh, the pain in those fathomlessly deep eyes. "You have nothing to apologize for. I'm glad you felt you could come here. I mean—"

"No, for this." He leaned toward me.

He was giving me warning.

All I had to do was pull back and make some smart-aleck remark. Make a joke. Tell a funny anecdote about what Claudia had done today at work.

But I didn't. I leaned toward him. My eyes drifted shut.

The first press of his lips was soft.

Soon, though, he grasped my cheek with his free hand.

When he nipped my lower lip, I opened up.

Eight years. For eight years, I'd pined for this untouchable man. For eight years, I believed he was straight.

More fool me.

He knew I was gay.

I'd come out of the closet at my high school graduation.

My parents hadn't batted an eye, and my grandmother embraced me and told anyone who'd listen—and even those who didn't want to hear.

On the job, I wore a pride baseball cap with a purple unicorn and the rainbow flag. I got dirty looks from some of our customers, but most were so grateful August'd fit them into the schedule that they weren't willing to risk upsetting the man.

In eight years, we'd only been asked to leave a job site once.

Whether the guy was bigoted about August being Black, me being gay, or some combination, I wasn't sure. And why I was thinking about that asshole while the most amazing man was sticking his tongue down my throat?

With my free hand, I ran my hand through his crinkly, short hair. I scratched his scalp—the way I knew he liked.

He groaned.

And pulled back.

Damn.

He met my gaze. "Can we take this to the bedroom?"

"Fuck, yes."

Wait, what does my bedroom look like?

I don't think he's going to care if your underwear is on the floor.

Good point.

"Yeah, let's go."

Chapter Two

August

This is so wrong.

Nia's dead.

Seize the day.

I should've been reluctant to enter Julian's bedroom. The guy's car was a disaster—with garbage shoved behind both the driver and passenger seats. I'd once glimpsed his trunk. Not good. But he kept my equipment in tip-top shape and had never once made a misstep.

Okay, except that tree on the Kittinger property, but really, they deserved it.

As he led me by the hand into his bedroom, I held my breath. I was really going to do this. Of course, I had no idea what *this* was. But whatever we did, it'd take my mind off Nia for a while. Anything. I'd do anything for a reprieve from the never-ending grief. And I probably shouldn't be making out while my sister was barely in the ground, but

I wanted to obliterate the memories of the past week. Julian could do that.

He released my hand as he moved swiftly to scoop up his work clothes and toss them into the closet, missing the laundry hamper. Only his pride hat remained, and he placed that carefully on his dresser.

Honestly, the room was neater than I imagined. And smelled of lavender. A scent I often used while trying to get to sleep.

His bed was unmade—not a surprise—but I didn't care. "Can I?" I pointed to my suit.

He nodded. Then he yanked his wrinkled white-cotton shirt over his head and made quick work of unzipping his jeans and yanking them down.

Commando.

Delicious.

Removing my clothes was a slower process. For reasons I couldn't fathom, I worn a suit and tie to Everett's office for the reading of the will.

He'd raised an eyebrow.

As I expected, I was the only person present. My best friend didn't care what I wore. His assistant, Tyrone, didn't care either. But I wanted to show respect for my sister—for what she represented to me.

Now, as I tore at my tie, I regretted the decision to go quite so formal. The day'd been so hot, and even moving swiftly from Everett's air-conditioned office to my air-conditioned car, I'd gotten overheated.

Speaking of overheated.

Julian, naked, was a sight to behold. The color differentiation of his farmer's tan was minute. He was religious about sunscreen and nagged the rest of us. His pale skin glowed in the light of the setting sun that fought its way through the sheers in the room. His hair was brown in the winter, but carried flecks of dark auburn after a season in the sun. And how would that adorable full beard feel rubbing against my skin?

My jacket and shirt came off, but if I didn't get out of these fucking pants, I'd never know. Naturally, my dress shoes had to come off first.

Shit, shit, shit.

Okay, breathe. I passed him and took a seat on the edge of the bed to undo the stubborn laces.

My heart leapt as he crawled onto the bed and behind me. He raked his fingers gently up and down my back, using his blunt, barely there fingernails. Was he arousing me or settling me? No clue, but I loved it. Shoes finally off, I yanked my socks down, then stood to pull off the pants. I was *not* commando, so I needed to pull down my underwear as well.

And even as I had the elastic in my hands, I hesitated.

I was about to be naked in front of a man. And not just any man. My employee. The man I'd fantasized about since the day I interviewed him for my fledgling company. The man who often appeared in my dreams. The man who was as far out of the closet as I was in it.

The man who sat back on his haunches and stroked his hard cock.

That should've reassured—that he wanted me as much as I wanted him. But wasn't this going too fast? Shouldn't we slow down and, you know, talk?

Seize the day.

With more guts than I knew I possessed, I yanked down my pants and briefs. I took a moment to fold the pants and lay them with the shirt and jacket on a chair. I had to leave here at some point, and having non-wrinkled clothes was important. And given I was a good six inches taller than Julian, and carried an extra twenty or thirty pounds, his clothes weren't likely to fit. We were both in shape. But while he was lean muscle, I was bulk.

When I stood, my own erection stuck out. I grasped it and squeezed, willing it to calm the fuck down. I was liable to come just from watching Julian as he continued his leisurely stroking.

"How do we... I mean, how does this...?"

Understanding flashed in his light-brown eyes. He understood. He wasn't going to make me say it.

Thank God.

He cleared his throat. "I've done it both ways. For a while, I was quite versatile. These days, I prefer topping." He licked his lips. "That being said, I'll take you any way I can get you."

"Yes, that. Please do that." Thank God he wasn't going to make me say it. Wasn't going to make me beg. For the first time, I wanted him in control. I'd be too worried about hurting him. Funny, I wasn't worried about him hurting me. I'd met several of his boyfriends over the years and none seemed unhappy. Not that you could tell, but I didn't figure they'd keep coming around if he was an inconsiderate lover. "Do you have..."

"If you can't say condoms and lube, I'm not sure we should be doing this."

Shit.

He winked.

I scowled.

Then he opened his bedside drawer and pulled out a strip of condoms and a bottle of lube. "I'd keep them out, but Mom's been known to drop by unannounced and set about cleaning the place. I know she wouldn't care, but I try to keep my embarrassment to a minimum."

I'd met his mother. Lovely woman. Pretty much the last person I wanted to be thinking of at this moment.

"So you'll fuck me?"

He patted the bed. "Oh, yeah. And it's going to be fucking amaz-ing."

Chapter Three

Julian

O kay, so August was coming to my bed. And I was going to fuck him.

Pretty much all my dreams come true.

I didn't want to think about what tomorrow would bring. Borrowing trouble, as Nana would say.

August climbed into bed as I scooted over to make space. He laid his head on the pillow and gazed up at me.

Ah, asking me to take the lead. This I could do. I stroked my hand down his clean-shaven jaw. Despite the manual labor involved in our job, his grooming was always meticulous. I was doing good to remember to trim my beard once a month.

I lazily drew my index finger down his throat, and he swallowed convulsively. I brushed past his pulse point and continued my exploration lower.

He startled when I tweaked his nipple. Less so when I did the other, but then he made a sound low in his throat when I took the bud in my mouth and nipped.

Nice.

His chest hair was sparse and coarse against my fingers. I'd never seen him without a shirt—but I'd suspected muscles.

I wasn't disappointed. Sculpted in all the right places, and sleek skin that rippled with my touch. I moved my hand down his stomach, swirling my finger in his belly button, and then meandered lower still.

I took his rock-hard erection in my hand, and he let out a strangled moan.

Stroking, I applied just the right amount of pressure.

He bucked.

I drew my tongue lazily down his flank, across his hipbone, and then I knelt before him and took his cock in my mouth.

His strangled cry lit a fire inside me.

Blow jobs came easily to me—been doing them since I was a teenager. As I sucked, I swirled my tongue around his length, taking the time to spear his slit.

He continued to emit inarticulate sounds of what I assumed was pleasure.

As I sucked harder, I had to hold his hips down as he undulated and tried to push into my mouth. I continued to use suction to draw every ounce of pleasure from him that I could manage. Need curled low in my belly as my erection begged for attention.

Fucker could wait. It'd be busy soon enough.

"I'm coming."

August's words were the only warning I got. I sucked harder as he spurted into my mouth. I swallowed the salty cum as best I could, wanting to give him an experience to remember. When he was limp, I pulled off him with a pop. I pressed a kiss to his cock and looked up his fantastic body to meet his gaze.

His glazed gaze. He was totally blissed out.

In that moment, I knew. I knew not only that he'd never done that before, but that I could fall hard for him if I wasn't careful. I crawled up his body and then covered it with my own. I thrust my tongue into his mouth and let him taste himself.

He roused enough to grasp my cheeks in his hands to hold me steady.

Then he raked his fingers through my beard. I loved that. I always did and I always would.

After a nice round of kissing, I pulled back. "You up for more?"

Those glazed eyes sharpened. "Always. With you? Always."

All the permission I needed. I snagged the bottle of lube. Oh good, practically full. Admittedly, I used lots of the stuff. I'd had more than a few lovers over the years and was very much into self-service. None of the guys lasted long because we hadn't formed an abiding connection. I could totally see that changing with August.

My boss.

Shut the fuck up.

Damn conscience.

On that note—less thinking, more action.

I crawled back down on him, and he naturally spread his thighs so I could settle between them. I placed my hands on his knees and he let them fall to the bed.

Before me lay the most beautiful sight. His balls were heavy. His hole was on full display. His cock lay limp, but I had hopes. He was only thirty-two. Maybe not a rangy teenager, but still had some vigor left in him. I wasn't doing so bad at thirty-nine. Able to hold an erection, as my cock reminded me.

After slathering my fingers with lube, I inched closer and leaned toward him.

He adjusted his thighs to part farther.

"Grab your knees."

His expression morphed from confusion to understanding, and he pulled his knees up.

I rubbed my fingers at the outside of his hole.

He tensed.

I continued.

He relaxed.

Slowly, with exquisite care, I slipped one finger in.

His eyes widened.

I wanted to ask if he'd ever done this before, but the moment felt too tenuous. Too fragile. And I didn't want to break his concentration. So I held his gaze as I added a second finger. I twisted, scissored, and then hit that spongy spot.

He gasped and his cock plumped just that little bit.

Nailed it.

Chapter Four

August

Okay. I knew where my prostate was. Knew how good it felt to touch it.

But having Julian do it brought my pleasure to a whole new level.

I could gaze into his gorgeous eyes forever, but I wanted more. My body demanded it as my cock plumped into a nice semi. I usually needed a decent refractory period, but just the thought of Julian inside me had my engines revving.

He withdrew his fingers, and I whimpered. As he sheathed his cock, though, an apprehension rippled through me. I had toys. In my mid-twenties, when I acknowledged I'd never act on my impulses toward men—especially not my employee who I daydreamed about all the time—I went into Vancouver and found a sex shop that catered to men like myself. I'd gone back a couple of times over the years and now had an impressive collection that I kept hidden in a box at the top of my walk-in closet—somewhere my petite sister could never reach. Not that she'd be nosy enough to do it.

Not that she'd ever do it now.

I ruthlessly shoved the flash of pain at her death back into the depths of my soul. I was about to get fucked. By Julian. I could deal with my anguish at her loss later.

"Are you...?"

"Fine. Just fine." I eyed his cock, now covered in the condom. "Now would be nice."

He grinned.

Happy was Julian's perpetual state of being. He was never without a quick quip, witty remark, or outright bawdy joke. Even after his beloved grandmother passed last year, he still relayed only fond remembrances of her. If he hurt, he did so in private.

"Okay. Grab your knees again."

I complied, pulling them out of the way and putting myself on full display for him.

His smile was a mile wide, and he flashed me a glimpse of those perfect teeth before he leaned forward. "This might hurt."

"I don't care." I really didn't. If it meant having what I'd wished for—waited for—all these years, I'd take it.

"Well, you've been warned." He winked as he lined himself up, then pressed in slowly. He levered himself above me, leaning on his elbows as he continued to slide in.

And it did hurt. But not unbearably so. The slow burn built, but then slowly receded as time passed. He seated himself fully, then he held himself still as I acclimated to the intrusion. I'd wanted this, and I had zero regrets.

Sweat broke out across his brow and I wiped it.

Our gazes clashed, and I nodded.

He nodded back and began to move. He pulled back a bit, then pushed back in.

I felt the slide. The pressure. The ache. All of it built in me as he continued to pull out almost all the way and push back inside.

He was holding back for me. "Fuck me, Julian. Please. Make me forget." The extent I was going to acknowledge anything other than the feel of him inside me.

"Okay." His thrusts became more insistent.

My cock perked up.

As he continued to nail me, he whispered, "Jack yourself. I want you to come again."

So, apparently, did my body. I smeared a bit of precum on my length and grasped my cock. I matched his rhythm stroke for stroke as I climbed higher and higher. I wanted to make this good for him, but holding on—holding out—felt impossible.

"Come." He spoke through gritted teeth. "It's okay to let go."

Letting go felt overwhelmingly impossible and absolutely necessary. So I did just that. I gave in and let the orgasm crash over me. I arched my neck and flung my head back as I let oblivion take over.

Julian thrust several more times, let out a few more oaths, and then he stilled.

I gazed up into his eyes as they blazed fire.

I caught my breath.

My life would never be the same.

Chapter Five

Julian

Not going to lie—the best sex ever.

And that was saying something. I'd enjoyed plenty of men over the years, but none had been so responsive. None had touched my soul. And I was pretty sure none had been a virgin.

I'd definitely been nervous.

But August's every reaction spurred me forward. Those little moans. The way he tightened around me. When he dug his heels into my hips to draw me closer. All of it took my breath away.

Now, as I came back down to earth from a mind-shattering orgasm, I reluctantly withdrew. I removed the condom, knotted it, and dropped it to the hardwood floor. I'd clean it up later.

The ceiling fan circulated the air, which was significantly warmer than when we first came in here. Generating a lot of body heat, apparently.

As I gathered August into my arms, I made a mental note of where the sheets were. Once we cooled, I might pull one over us. Of course, what were a few goose bumps if it meant I could gaze at this perfection? Even as I had the thought, I pushed it aside. He wouldn't like that. If I knew one thing about my boss, it was that looks didn't matter to him. He never objectified and he wouldn't want to be.

I lay on my back and encouraged him to roll toward me and rest his head in the crook of my arm.

He complied and then drew lazy circles across my abdomen. I wasn't as taut as I'd been fifteen years ago, but I was in decent shape. Climbing trees to trim them all day kept me in good shape. If I had a cheeseburger once in a while, I wasn't likely to pay for it. Ten or fifteen years from now, that might be a different story.

"She's gone."

I stroked his head, using my nails to scratch his scalp. "I know."

"And I wasn't there."

"Even if you had been, there's nothing you could've done. She died in her sleep. Peaceful. The way we all wish to go, I think." Surely he could draw some solace from that. Right? I didn't know.

"There are so many things I wished I'd said."

"She knew you loved her. I remember you telling me that you thanked her once for taking care of you. And you returned the favor over the years." I could think of a dozen or more times he'd visited her house to help. She'd chosen an older home in an established neighborhood. Naturally, she constantly needed things done, and August'd always been willing to help.

"But I never told her about…" He pressed his hand to my belly.

My stomach dropped. Was that why he was here? Because with Nia dead, he could finally be with a man and not feel guilt? Had I even factored into the equation, or was I just the lucky guy he decided to use to lose his virginity?

His head snapped as he looked up at me.

I hadn't said anything, but apparently my body language had done the talking for me.

"No." His eyes widened. "It's not like that." He rotated and pressed up so our faces were nose to nose. His eyes were intense as he met my gaze. "I've wanted you for-fucking-ever. Was her death the impetus for me to find the courage to come here? Yes. I want to believe I would've found the courage." He swallowed. Hard. "When Everett read the will..."

A tear slipped from his eye, and I wiped it away as it trailed down his cheek.

"She knew. Right in the will, she said she knew. She said she regretted that I'd never felt comfortable coming out, but that she hoped I'd one day find the courage." He sniffled. "And she said she thought I didn't come out because I was worried about her and about the business, and if she was gone—because why else would I be reading her will—then she was leaving me the means and permission to come out."

I frowned. "What does that mean?"

He blinked. "Right. You probably want to know what her will stipulates."

"If you want to share." I cupped his cheek. "But it's none of my business. You had a special relationship with your sister, and I have no claim over you."

"Well, I might as well tell you." He cleared his throat. "Remember that app I told you about last year? The one that blocks robocalls?"

I had some vague memory of him forcing me to install something on my phone. Well, forcing was too strong a word. Encouraging vociferously might be a better way to put it. "Sure. You said it was the best thing ever invented. I mean, I'm not getting any more spam calls, so I guess you're right. I haven't thought about it much."

"Well, I didn't know this, but Nia invented it."

This time, I blinked. I'd known she was a computer programmer and... Nope, that was about all I knew. "So she invented this thing?"

He nodded. "And sold it. For over a billion dollars."

Holy shit. I couldn't fathom that kind of money. I mean, I'd heard about rich tech entrepreneurs, but I didn't know anyone. I thought Nia just, I don't know, fixed things or something. But creating something that was helpful to hundreds of millions, if not billions, of people around the world? My mind was appropriately blown. "She never told you."

"No, she didn't." His eyes flashed with that hurt. "It's not like I would've asked her for any of it or anything like that."

"You're not that kind of brother, and I'm sure Nia knew it."

"Yeah." He placed a hand over my heart. Was he even aware of the gesture?

"What did her will say?" I didn't really have the right to know, but obviously this weighed on my friend.

"She left it all to me. I'm now a billionaire."

The words made little sense. The August in my arms was the same man I'd always known. Okay, I hadn't known he was gay—but the rest was just him. I didn't see him any differently. "What're you going to do?"

"Nia left a list of charities. She wants me to create a foundation and give grants each year. She's even named a woman who can help me—Emma-Jane Ward—who has experience with these things. Nia left the final decision up to me, but she encouraged me to consider this. Apparently she had plans to do this, and had done some preliminary work. Everett gave me the password so I can access her files." He met my gaze. "I don't know if I want the responsibility. I just want to live my life the way I always have. I love trees. I love working with nature."

"Then contact Ms. Ward and ask her to take over. I'm sure you can take on a figurehead role. Do what Nia wanted without changing who you are." I pulled him close and pressed a kiss to his lips. "Because you're perfect just the way you are."

He eyed me. "Eight years was a long time to wait."

I barked out a laugh. "If I'd known, I'd have jumped your bones years ago. But you needed to make peace, and now I think you've done it. Nia told you to be your authentic self. I say go for it."

"And you'll be by my side."

My heart sang. "Count on it."

He pressed our lips together. "I love you. I always have, and I always will."

"Same goes. And just so you know, I loved you long before now. Trust me, I'm not in it for the money."

We sealed our love with another kiss.

One story to go! Harold and Derek might meet in Merritt, BC, but the story has ties to Mission City...

Ace's Place

A Mission City Gay Romance Short Story

Gabbi Grey

Derek Murphy has come to the godforsaken small town of Merritt, British Columbia in search of a new beginning. The man is tired, jaded, and resigned to never having sex again. Until Friday night at the local sports bar changes everything.

Harold Graham, hometown boy made good, has lived in Merritt his entire life. When he meets the new guy in town, he's compelled to reach out the hand of friendship. And maybe more.

But secrets and omissions cloud what could be the beginning of something special. Can they take a chance on being vulnerable enough to fall in love?

Ace's Place is a 13k word short story about second-chances, hockey, and an adorable but nosy Bouvier.

Contents

Chapter One

Derek

From the outside, the place looked like a dive, and the inside wasn't much better.

You're being pretentious. And picky.

Two things I could no longer afford to be. The chain hotel I was staying at had decent room-service food, but I needed something more. Something greasy, filling, and bad for my arteries. To hasten my demise in this God-awful small town. If boredom didn't kill me first.

Ace's Place. The only sports bar in Merritt, British Columbia. Better known as the middle of fucking nowhere.

Okay, that might have been an exaggeration. The town had over seven thousand residents. It was on the Trans-Canada Highway, so if one was going from Vancouver to, I don't know, Calgary, one would travel through this backwater town. Unfortunately, I wasn't traveling to Calgary. Or Toronto or Montréal or anywhere urban and urbane.

Nope, Merritt was the last stop for me. An ignominious end to what had begun as a very glorious career.

In the past.

Now I was about to hunker down for a meal at this bar. Ace's Place wasn't the only bar within the boundaries of Merritt, but as it was next to my hotel, it won. I could drink myself into oblivion, and only have to walk a couple hundred feet back to the semi-comfortable bed that awaited me.

Three days. I'd been here for three days and I was already numb. What would I be like after three months? Three years? Hell, three decades? A shell of my former self. Guaran-fucking-teed.

I opened the door, and the smell of beer and fried food assailed me. Reminded me of the bar back in Vancouver I used to frequent with my co-workers after we quit on Friday nights. A far cry from the gay bars I haunted on Saturday night. Those forays, I kept to myself.

A young woman in a black shirt and short black skirt approached me. I held up one finger before she could get a word in edgewise.

"Bar or table?"

A decision almost too much to deal with, but I answered. "Bar." No need to occupy an entire table. The place was hopping with almost every booth filled.

"Game night." She answered my unasked question as she led me to the bar.

I selected the stool at the end and slid onto it.

After she handed me a menu, she headed off.

I perused the menu. Perfect, there were hardly any healthy items on it.

A coaster was placed in front of me, and I glanced up to see who'd put it there.

My breath caught.

Dark-brown hair. Shaved at the sides, longer on top. Sexy trimmed scruff. And the deepest-brown eyes I'd ever seen. Oh, and the body? I tried to be circumspect in my examination but, man, he made my mouth water. Brawny, but not beefy. Wide shoulders with muscular arms. His black T-shirt was tight across his broad chest.

He was scrumptious enough to eat.

And by his raised eyebrow, I'd taken just a moment too long in my perusal.

Crap.

"Whatever you have on tap."

"We have eight brews." He named all eight.

I tried not to think that my old pub had a much larger selection.

"The pale ale would be great."

He nodded and moved over to the tap. As he poured, I watched him instead of the beer. The movement of his arm, the furrow of concentration in his brow, the flexing of his abs when he hit the right amount of beer and foam. My cock sat up and took notice—something that hadn't happened in a very long time.

"One pale ale." His eyes sparkled in the light from the upper frame of the bar. "You decide on food?"

"Greasy, please." I handed him the menu. "And spicy."

His grin did things to my stomach. "One jalapeño burger with a side of spicy mushroom caps. That'll fill your belly."

Said stomach growled. How long since I'd eaten? Food? A few hours. A man like him? Way too fucking long. He was so my type. And probably as straight as they came.

I sipped my beer as I watched him work the bar. Beer was flowing, and I quickly picked up it was hockey night. Apparently the home-town junior team was playing, as every screen in the place was tuned to the game. I liked hockey as much as most Canadians, and being a hometown Vancouverite, I enjoyed Canucks games. That being said, I only attended when work gave me tickets. I had season tickets for the symphony.

Didn't figure that'd go over well in this crowd.

"One jalapeño burger and one side of spicy mushroom caps. Anything else I can get you?"

He'd caught me unawares. *You* probably wouldn't go over well in this crowd either.

"No, this is great. Smells delicious." And it did. Better than the BLT sandwich I'd had for lunch.

He placed a rolled napkin with all the cutlery, winked, and backed away. Before I could say another word, he was halfway down the bar and leaning over so he could hear the server giving him a drink order.

A wink?

Because the food was good, or because he read something more? Was there longing in my expression? My last hookup had been over six months ago. Longest dry spell since I'd turned nineteen and could head to the gay bars down on Davie Street. I'd taken full advantage over the past ten years. Always being safe, but enjoying myself nonetheless. Nothing serious, though. No, nothing to distract from my career.

What a fucking joke that turned out to be. Not lost on me what I'd missed out on.

I bit into the burger and moaned. Juice dribbled down my chin, and I quickly swiped it up with the napkin. Holy Lord. I couldn't remember the last time I'd had anything this good. Maybe ever. After chewing thoroughly, I swallowed, took a swig of beer, then popped a mushroom cap into my mouth. Heaven. I'd died and gone to heaven.

All in Ace's Place.

The bartender returned and pointed to the food.

"Amazing," I enthused. "Hey, what's your name?"

A sly grin cut across his expression. "Harold."

"Harold?" He didn't look like a Harold.

"Better known as... Harold." Swiping the cloth across the bar, he offered a sheepish smile. "I wanted Harry or, I don't know, anything other than Harold. But my great-grandfather carried the name, and he died in the war, so my mother insisted on honoring him. I think she did it to curry favor with my grandfather. Whatever. It's just a name, though." Another swipe against the pristinely clean mahogany. "What's your name?"

"Derek."

Harold nodded. "And where do you hail from, Derek? Because I know just about everyone in town, and I don't know you. Or are you passing through our fair city?"

I wish.

"I'm from the coast. I just took a job teaching at the community college. I start Monday."

Another nod. "Yeah, Ms. Caulder's sudden heart attack devastated the entire town. Just six months from retirement, no less." He pointed at me. "Guess they were lucky you could come up here so fast. Vancouver, right?"

Since I was pretty sure I didn't have a Vancouver accent, he'd likely made an educated guess. I supposed I could've come from elsewhere, but what was the point of attempting subterfuge? Yes, I was starting over. No, I didn't have anything to hide.

"Yeah, Vancouver." Point Grey, to be exact. The most exclusive neighborhood in the city. Or that's where my parents lived. I'd had a condo in the downtown core. One I'd just sold for an obscene amount of money. I pointed to the plate which held only remnants of one of the best meals I'd ever consumed. "Amazing."

"We do our best. Got a great kitchen staff." He organized the plates into a pile. "You want another drink? Maybe some desert? We've got a decadent cheesecake."

I patted my flat belly. Wouldn't stay that way if I indulged too often. "I'm good. I might hang for a bit before heading back to my hotel."

He cocked his head in the direction whence I'd come.

"Yep. Just until Friday. I got a great deal on a house in Bench. Four bedrooms and three bathrooms for less than my one-bedroom condo in downtown Vancouver cost."

Another nod. "Yeah, we get lots of city folks settling up here. Not too far of a drive, but far enough away that real estate prices haven't gotten silly. With telecommuting these days, people can live everywhere. Our small community is expanding with city slickers getting away from the rat race."

"You always live here?"

"Five generations. My family used to own the general store back in the day. We've held various jobs over the years, nothing sticking. My two younger sisters headed to Vancouver and never looked back. Small town living never suited them."

"But it did you?" That fascinated me.

A huge grin. "Big fish in a small pond."

I was about to ask what he meant when a guy sauntered up to the bar. He pointed to the stool next to me, and I gestured for him to have at it.

He plopped down, removed his baseball cap, and set it on the stool next to him. "Cold one, please."

"Sure, West. Rough day?"

The guy shrugged. "I caught three kids smoking dope behind the school when they were supposed to be in my gym class. Instead of turning them in, I made them run continuous laps until the period ended. Two of them threw up, and the third collapsed."

Harold raised an eyebrow.

West waved him off. "All for show, I promise. They showered, rehydrated, and went on to English. I suspect it'll be a long time before they smoke weed instead of coming to my class."

The man looked on the young side to be a teacher. I didn't peg him for much more than twenty-five. Of course I was only twenty-nine, but I felt decades older. His light-brown hair was much shorter than my light blond. He had almost a buzz cut—close to the look I used to sport—but I hadn't been to a hairdresser in six months. And his eyes were a stunning hazel. I'd been told my sky-blue eyes were my best feature, but I wasn't convinced of that. I always figured guys used it as a line.

"West, this here is Derek. He's new in town. Derek, this is West. Used to play for the Junior A team, and he decided to stick around. Now he's the gym teacher at the high school."

We shook hands. His grip was powerful, but something in his expression caught my attention.

"You from the Lower Mainland?"

Sheesh, what was everyone's obsession about where I came from? "Yes, Vancouver."

"Ah." He grabbed the beer Harold presented him. "Just wondered if you might've been out in Mission City or Abbotsford."

An odd question. But that ghosted look flashed again. Obviously something was prompting the curiosity. More likely, someone.

"Can't say I made it out to the Fraser Valley often. Worked and lived downtown."

"Fair enough." He took a long drink, then turned to the bartender. "Plate of nachos, hold the jalapeños."

Harold glanced my way when he said, "You two will never be compatible."

West snorted, cutting a glance my way. "I take it you like those little fuckers." He took another sip of beer. "And I don't play for that team." His brow furrowed. "Not that there's anything wrong with that. I mean—"

"You're talking too much, Mr. Harris. Drink your beer."

Saluting Harold with his beer, West snickered. "Never let an excellent brew go to waste." He took a long draw. "What is it you do, Derek?"

"He's taking up the teaching job at the community college."

Would I be allowed to contribute to the conversation?

West turned to give me a good look. "Glad you're here. Those kids deserve the best instructors."

"I don't know if I'm the best—"

"You're here and you're breathing. I assume you have some business background..."

"MBA and CPA." Said with little thought. I didn't need to defend my credentials. I didn't have any teaching experience, but I knew the material inside and out.

"The student body is a huge cross-section of students from the surrounding area."

Ah, I saw where he was going with this. "I'm aware of the make-up of the students. You don't need to worry about me." In other words, I wasn't a bigot. I could honestly trot out the standard *I have Indigenous friends* line but it'd be trite. One of my best friends at the university had been from a reserve in Northern British Columbia. She'd fought long and hard to get into the Sauder School of Business. She now ran the finance department for her entire region. Had I witnessed discrimination against her? Yes. Had I spoken up? Also, yes. But she said she preferred to fight her own battles. It just pissed me off she had to at all.

Harold dropped a huge steaming plate of nachos in front of West. "Eat up, my friend, because I'm going to kick your ass Sunday morning."

West grunted, took a huge mouthful, then cringed and took a swig of beer. "Jesus, buddy."

"You think I wouldn't bring them right out of the oven?" Bartender grinned. "Best in town."

"Best in the Nicola Valley." West blew on a chip before popping it in his mouth. He finished chewing, took another swig of beer, and tipped his glass. "And we're going to kick your ass Sunday morning."

"There's going to be ass kicking?" I was intrigued.

"Hockey, to be precise." West blew on another chip, and I was forced to wait as he ate. At least he didn't speak with his mouth full. "We play hockey most Sunday mornings. Bright and early."

Harold returned with a full sleeve of beer and put it in front of me, taking away my half-full glass. Or was that half-empty?

"Lukewarm sucks ass."

"You would know, buddy." Another chip. West must've been starving by the way he devoured that meal.

"I think you mean suck cock and kiss ass." Harold again winked at me, then sauntered down to the far end of the bar, where he served several beers in bottles.

Had he just...?

West cleared his throat. "Uh, I sure hope you bat for that team or this might get awkward."

"I...uh..."

He waved. "This is a pretty progressive town, and I work with a lesbian teacher. The principal of the elementary school is gay, the mayor has a trans son, and the head reporter at the paper did a byline about how inclusivity benefits everyone. Someone painted a rainbow crosswalk and life's been pretty sweet. Does it help that the hometown hero son is gay? Yeah, probably."

"Harold."

West cut me a bemused glance. "Oh, Harold, is it? That'd thrill his mother. I've met the woman more than a few times. Don't cross her. She's a sedate lady most of the time, but piss her off and she's a wild cat." He eyed a chip with cheese dripping off it. "She's shorter and stouter, but she looks exactly like, uh, Harold. Works as a greeter at the supermarket. That way she keeps up with all the latest gossip."

Good to know. I didn't plan to seek Mrs., uh, what was Harold's last name? Anyway, I wasn't planning to seek the woman out, but I suspected in this small town we might just run into each other. And I had to ask, "why do you keep stumbling on Harold's name?"

The man next to me snickered. "Because none of us call him Harold. He's hiding something from you—and far be it for me to give his secret away—but he's up to something. I'd warn you to watch out, but you're from the city. You seem pretty smart, so I suspect you can take care of yourself."

I wasn't certain if I'd just been insulted or complimented. "You're not from around here?"

He shook his head. "Abbotsford born and bred." He dropped the nacho in what I could only term disgust. "Nothing left for me there. I finished teacher's college and decided to make Merritt my home. I've done all right for myself."

"More than all right." Harold had reappeared in time to pick up the half-empty plate. "To go?"

West nodded.

"Hey, is Zach coming up for Sunday's game?"

West checked his watch. "He's due in about an hour. I'm meeting him at my place. We've got coaching in the morning, which is why I'm done." He'd barely drunk half his beer.

"Coach and a player?"

"I coach half-a-dozen sports at the high school as well as a junior hockey team in town. Pretty talented kids. Some of them are going places, you know? I had dreams of making it big, but I was never good enough. Didn't have the fire in the belly. Now I try to inspire kids to be better than I was. Not to put too much pressure on them, though. I want them to enjoy the game."

He tossed his credit card onto the bar and Harold whipped it away, coming back within moments with the receipt and the boxed nachos.

West signed the receipt and saluted me. "You'll do all right here, Derek. Feel free to drop by the rink on Sunday mornings if you're bored. A bunch of old geezers playing for fun."

Neither West nor Harold fit the description of *old geezer*, but I understood what he was saying. He rose, stretched, nodded once, and ambled out.

Harold was there within moments, grabbing the beer glass.

The entire bar erupted in applause, hoots, and cheers. There'd been the odd noise before, but this far eclipsed anything else.

Harold grinned. "Hot damn. Those kids are amazing. Four to one. Decent score, and now they're in contention. They win the next two and they're guaranteed a spot." He glanced around. "This place'll be chaos. Our best time of year is always playoffs."

I avoided sports bars when the Canucks were in the finals. I liked camaraderie as much as the next guy, but I also enjoyed hearing myself think. Sipping my beer, I took stock of the situation. Going home alone to the hotel room held little appeal, but did I have a reason to stay?

Before I could come up with an appropriate answer, Harold leaned over and beckoned me close. "I'm off in an hour. I could keep you company tonight, if you're interested. Because I do believe we're on the same team."

My cheeks heated, and I glanced around, but no one was paying us any mind. They were still all clapping and cheering the win.

On impulse, I pulled the second key card from my wallet. "Room 302. Bring supplies."

Chapter Two

Derek

B ring supplies?

How pathetic did that make me? I could've run to the local drugstore to buy supplies. I'd tossed out what few I had left before I'd moved up here, believing I'd never need them again. Consigned myself to celibacy because how the hell was I going to meet another gay man in a town this small? And how would the college feel if they knew I was gay?

Apparently two incredibly naïve questions. Seemingly no one batted an eye at teachers and administrators being gay, and surprisingly, I was able to get picked up on my first foray into town.

Pretty impressive.

I paced the length of the room back and forth. About twelve feet. I wanted to go for a run to blow off some steam. I used to run around English Bay every morning before a hot shower and a coffee on my way to the office. Routine. I was a creature of routine.

And I hadn't run in six months. Not since the day they fired me.

Stop thinking.

About that or about everything? Because if I reflected on what I'd agreed to, thinking was kind of important. I'd invited a virtual stranger to my hotel room. I didn't do stuff like that. The guys I hooked up with? Always their place or at an anonymous hotel. I'd never brought a guy home and yes, for argument's sake, this hotel wasn't my home. But this room was my sanctuary until I took possession of my new house in six days.

The hot, sexy bartender was on his way over.

If he doesn't stand you up.

I waved off that thought. Harold was obviously well known. He didn't seem like the kind of guy who'd jeopardize his reputation by stiffing the new guy in town. In fact, if pressed, I'd say he was the kind of guy everyone loved. The kind who took strangers under his wings and protected them. The kind of guy I could come to care for.

The polar opposite of everyone who'd fucked me in the last ten years.

And been fucked, I quickly added. I'd done some fucking in my early days. Experimentation, mostly. Wasn't really my thing.

A quick rap on the door caught me mid-stride, and before I could react, the key card was inserted in the lock, which clicked open. Harold slipped into the room and let the door swish quietly closed behind him. He met my gaze, and his grin widened.

I'd changed into jeans and a T-shirt from my more formal khakis and button-down, but something told me that wasn't the reason for the grin. He nodded toward my bare feet.

"Interesting choice in the middle of February."

"The room was warm. And..." I curled my toes. "I saw the movie *Die Hard*, and it's true that if you curl your toes into the carpet that you relax. I used to do it every night when I came home from work. Nightcap and toe curling."

Was I a tad defensive?

Harold snickered. "I just think feet are really sexy. Loved *Die Hard*. Best Christmas movie ever."

A chink in my armor.

"You mind if I take my coat off?"

"Of course not. Please make yourself at home. Would you like a beer?"

He shucked off his coat and hung it over the desk chair, then advanced farther into the room. He casually dropped a strip of condoms and a small bottle of lube on the bed. "I'm not much for beer, but you feel free."

I swallowed hard, pushing down the nerves fluttering in my stomach. "I don't need alcohol. Just trying to be a good host."

He stilled. "Look, Derek, we don't have to do this. There's no rush. You're new in town, and likely going to be here a while. I'm never leaving and, despite what you may hear, am not a player."

"That's not what West implied."

"Jesus." He raked a hand through his hair. "West is...he can be cocky and he can be melancholy. The one thing he is, however, is honest. Have I played around in the past? When I was younger, sure. Those days are behind me. I'm not saying I want forever with you, but I'll take what I can get. You intrigue me. Can't say that about most people in town these days."

Something inside me snapped. In a good way. I covered the six-foot distance in two long strides and planted myself before him. He had a good five inches on me, but he only needed to lower his head a bit for our gazes to lock. Blazing fire lit those dark-brown irises. Oh yeah, this was going to be good.

He raised his hand tentatively to cup my cheek.

I leaned into the touch, allowing him to sweep his large thumb against my lips.

"I want to devour you."

"I want to be devoured." *Less talk, more action please.*

"Are you saying...?"

Well, might as well be honest. "I prefer to bottom, but at this point it's been so long, I'm willing to do just about anything.

He chortled. "It's been a long time for me as well, and I prefer to top, so I think we're going to be just fine." He leaned forward and kissed me gently on the lips.

Fuck this.

I grabbed the back of his head and tugged him down to me. I nipped at his bottom lip, and when he opened, I thrust my tongue inside. I didn't want sweet. I didn't want gentle. I wanted life-affirming passion and downright dirty sex. All the hearts and flowers shit could come later.

And something told me there *would* be a later.

He grabbed the hem of my T-shirt and we broke the kiss only long enough to yank it off. He tossed it away and our mouths were already fused again when he raked his fingernails across my abs.

Fuck that felt good.

I undid his belt buckle as he toed off his shoes. We broke the kiss and our gazes locked.

"You do you, I'll do me, and let's meet on the bed in about twenty seconds."

I liked his plan. I pulled my jeans and briefs off in one smooth motion and tossed them on the floor with my T-shirt. After putting the lube and condoms on the bedside table, I pulled back the covers and hopped into bed. My earlier excuse about having taken my socks off because the room was warm wasn't accurate. I kept the heat low, and the sheets were cool, but my blood was heated. Watching Harold yank his shirt over his head, pull down his jeans and briefs, then wrench off his socks was one of the sexiest shows I'd ever seen.

Dark hair covered his chest, tapering off as it went lower. Those arms were solid, as were those muscular thighs. And his cock? A thing of beauty. Half-hard and arrowed down, I spotted impressive girth. I licked my lips.

He pressed a knee to the bed and levered himself so he could crawl up to me. He held himself steady above me until I gave him a slight nod. Reading it for the consent it was, he lowered himself so he lay on top of me. Completely covering me.

I'd never felt so protected. So cherished.

I spread my thighs to invite him closer, and when our cocks brushed, electricity shot through me. This time he nipped at my lower lip, and I opened for him, greedy and needy. His exploration of my mouth was downright carnal, and as he ground our cocks together, I grew harder. I ran my hands through his hair, finding it much softer than I would've imagined. Curling my fingers around his neck, I drew him even closer.

Would he devour me?

Could he devour me?

I wanted to find out.

Boldly, I trailed my fingers down his torso and drew them across his abs and down farther. When I grasped him intimately, he sucked in a breath, pulling back from our kiss. "Keep that up and it'll be over way too soon."

It tempted part of me to tease him, but this moment felt too precious. Too fragile. Something in him called to something in me, and bold was the only way I knew to proceed.

"I want you inside me when you come. I need to feel you."

His eyes blazed that same fire I'd spotted earlier. He let out a shaky breath. "I usually build to this."

Was I pushing too hard? What if I blew this before it'd even begun? I was playing by a new rule book here, and the regulations weren't clear to me. I didn't want him to call foul before we'd even started.

He pressed a kiss to my forehead. "I want to be inside you. I just don't want to go too far and have nowhere left to go."

Pressing my groin against his, I assured him. "I have a significant repertoire. We'll never run out of things to do."

His grin was downright lascivious. "Okay then." He rolled to his side, then reached over for the lube. He handed it to me. "Show me."

I spread my legs, then lubed up my fingers. I moved my cock and balls out of the way so my hole was on full display. This time, he licked his lips. I pressed my index finger inside, feeling both disconnected and connected. Disconnected because it'd been so fucking long, and connected because something passed between the two of us. I'd dissect it later for meaning, but for now, I added a second finger and curled them, seeking my pleasure spot.

Given I loved bottoming, I was well-acquainted with my prostate. When I hit the spongy spot, pleasure sang through my veins. My cock leaked precum on my stomach, and I was mighty pleased when Harold fumbled with the wrapper as he opened it. He rolled the condom on and it took mere moments for him to slather on the lube. "How do you want me?"

"On top." I didn't always choose this position, especially if I didn't know the guy well, but I wanted to feel his weight, needed to cede the control to him. I trusted him. God only knew why, but he engendered trust.

Might be a bartender thing.

Might be a Harold thing.

Didn't matter. I spread my thighs for him and guided him to me.

He was on the big side, and I was on the tight side, but something about the burn brought me back to life. I remembered not only why I liked sex, but how it grounded me. Connected me. Invigorated me. As he pressed in slowly, I gazed into those beautiful eyes. His pupils were blown wide in the low light of the room. I'd only left one light on because as much as I wanted to see him, I also felt exposed in a way I hadn't for a long time. He could see into my soul and, in that moment, I wasn't sure I wanted to know what he saw.

"Fuck, you're tight." He continued to push in, finally seating himself fully. "You okay, Derek?"

I squeezed him experimentally. Not only revelling in the fullness, but assuring him I was okay. I was more than okay. I was alive, he was glorious, and now I wanted to be pounded into the mattress. Being in a hotel made the whole affair both more illicit and more fun. If he rode me hard enough, would the neighbors hear?

"Please, Harold, make me feel. Take me away from this place."

He looked momentarily uncertain, so I wrapped my legs around his hips and drew him into me as best I could. I wanted to ask for more, but this was our first time.

Hopefully there'd be a second. And a third. But I wasn't greedy—I'd take whatever he was willing to give.

Flexing his hips, he continued to hold my gaze. Withdraw and thrust. Move back and press forward. I wanted to beg him to go faster and harder, but he needed to do this at his pace. And I was no longer the man who could make those demands. I was a desperate man, understanding the grace that brought us together on this cold winter night.

"You feel so fucking good. I want to last but..." His words died on a hard thrust.

"Do it." I urged him, pleading with my eyes. "Only you can give me this."

Truer words were never spoken. He withdrew then pushed into me so deep I knew I'd be feeling it tomorrow. Making me whole. I squeezed him, and he finally seemed to get the message. The tempo picked up, settling us into a punishing rhythm. What I'd wanted but hadn't known how to ask for. He pounded, I received, and we made some kind of special magic. He hit my prostate unerringly over and over, and soon I was the one cresting.

"I'm going to come." Sweat broke across my brow, and my thighs trembled with the force of holding him close.

"Do it." He moved in for a brief but brutal kiss. "Jack yourself. Do whatever you need to do. Just make it quick."

Sweat broke out across his brow as he gritted his teeth.

I needed no further urging. I took myself in hand, spread some precum along my length, and jacked myself to the punishing and unrelenting rhythm he set.

His urging and permission were all I needed. My balls drew up, and I let go.

As my cum spurted between the two of us, he thrust twice more and then he followed me over.

"Christ, yes." The words escaped him on a long exhalation. His head was arched back and the cords of his neck bulged. Then he looked down at me and our gazes met. The moment suspended in time. A connection I felt to the marrow of my bones. Something I never wanted to end.

He continued to prop himself up on his elbows, but clearly the effort was getting to be too much. I wound my arms around his neck and pulled him close. He collapsed onto me.

The weight was glorious. I wasn't a small man by any extent of the imagination, but I wasn't big like him. Yet his weight didn't suffocate me. Far from it. His mere presence reassured me that life would move on. That I'd move on.

Might I be so lucky as to move on with him?

Too fanciful, and likely the thought was being caused by my sex-haze-induced euphoria. Yet when he swept my damp hair away from my face, I knew we had cemented a connection.

Chapter Three

Derek

Harold was the first to move, easing himself gently from me, then rolling out of bed. He grazed his hand along my hip before heading to the bathroom.

The water ran, and soon he was back with a washcloth. He sat on the bed, met my gaze, and pressed the warm cloth against my belly.

More intimate than any act I'd ever had done to me before.

He'd removed the condom, and he did a quick swipe of his own belly, wiping away my cum. After placing the cloth on the bedside table, he rolled into bed, and lay on his back. His arm went around my shoulder as he urged me to roll into his embrace. I pulled the sheet and blanket over us and laid my head on his chest. The crinkly hair against my unshaven chin created an odd friction.

I drew lazy, random patterns across his sexy abs. Yes, he was a damn fine-looking man, but I sensed great depth.

"What are you running from?"

His softly spoken words caught me off guard. I'd thought we might engage in pillow talk. Plan our next tryst—if there was to be one—exchange favorite position notes.

Hell, what did I know? I was the one who was usually out the door within an hour. Grab a cab home, have a quick shower, settle in for the night. I didn't do...whatever this was.

"I'm not running." I tried to keep the defensiveness from my tone.

"Try again." He feathered his fingers through my hair. "If you don't want to tell me, that's okay." He sighed. "But I'd like to do this again, and I feel truth is important. You're hiding something, and maybe it's none of my business—"

"—it's not—"

"—but I like to know where I stand."

I grazed my knuckles against his cock. The hand gripping my shoulder tightened.

"Tell me why you're running."

"I'm not—"

But I stopped myself. *If* this was going to become a thing, and *if* we had a future, I had to be brutally honest with him.

"I'm not running. Was I chased away? Maybe." I swallowed the lump in my throat that always lodged there. "You have to understand, I grew up with my grandparents after my parents died in a boating accident when I was three. I have no memory of my folks."

He made a sound low in his throat. Probably sympathy, but I knew I had to keep going. "I loved them, but they were much older, and I knew soon I'd have to make my own way in the world. I studied like crazy and got into business school at the University of British Columbia. I earned my CPA status and did an MBA. By the time I graduated, my grandparents had passed.

"But I was doing okay. I took a job with a firm I'd done a study semester with. A boutique accounting firm in downtown Vancouver who catered to the wealthiest of clients. I set my sights on making partner by the time I hit thirty-five. And I was well on my way."

He rubbed his hand up and down my arm. Was he sensing my growing discomfort? I didn't want to continue, but I had to.

"One night I was working late—a common occurrence—and I found a stack of papers in the copy room on the printer. I checked to see who they belonged to. One of the senior partners. She was my mentor, and I worked on all her files, so it surprised me she had a client I didn't know about.

"I know what I did was wrong, but I was curious. I perused. And then read. And then delved." I swallowed. "I stayed all night reviewing the account, and by morning I had irrefutable proof she was engaging in...well I want to say shady business practices, but what she was doing was flat-out wrong. She'd created a scheme so her client could move his money offshore and avoid paying significant taxes. Everything they were doing was illegal. Immoral. If they got caught, both of them would be in serious trouble."

I scrubbed my face. "And the kicker? The client was obscenely wealthy. He had more than enough money to pay taxes, and plenty of loopholes existed for him to drive a truck through. But instead of paying his fair share, he was looking for a way to cheat the system. And my boss'd given it to him."

"What did you do?" He asked it quietly. Unobtrusively.

"I confronted her the next morning." I laid my hand flat across his stomach, absorbing some of the warmth into my icy fingers. It couldn't have been comfortable for him, but he didn't complain. "She tried to tell me I was wrong. That I didn't know what I was doing.

When she saw she couldn't persuade me, she tried to bring me in on the deal."

"Did you consider it?"

"For a nanosecond. She was offering me big bucks. But the thought of being complicit was too much. I threatened to go to the other partners, and she fired me. On the spot. Threatened me too. Said if I ever told anyone, she'd get me blacklisted. I'd never work in Vancouver again."

Harold stiffened. "I take it you didn't hold your peace."

"Oh fuck, no. I went to the other partners, and when they shut me down, I placed an anonymous tip to the fraud line with the tax department. It quickly became apparent they needed my testimony, and I figured...well, why stop now? She'd already blacklisted me, so I did what I needed to do. And yes, I'd acted illegally when I took those papers, but the government was happy to overlook that fact. They raided the offices, and despite the best efforts of the partners, the government discovered schemes for dozens of clients.

"Within a month, it all fell apart." God, he smelled good. His scent was lulling me. "All the dominos fell. I, uh, have to go back to testify. Unless they all take a plea deal. The clients are claiming they didn't know the scheme was illegal, and the accountants have hired expensive lawyers, but they're facing the revocation of their licence to practice." I closed my eyes. "And, yes, they blacklisted me. Several firms considered hiring me, especially because of my high ethics, but I was just too toxic. The job opened up here, and I took it."

"You'll be doing a lot of good."

"I hope so. I really do. If this winds up being transitional, I guess that'd be okay. But, truthfully, I'm ready to settle down."

My hand grazed his cock again.

"Much as I'd love to go again, I'm not twenty, and Benjamin's waiting at home."

I stiffened. He had a boyfriend at home? I didn't like the feeling in the pit of my stomach. I didn't do cheating. Probably my only hard-and-fast rule.

He gently eased me away, and something inside me snapped. "You know the way out. I need a shower."

"Hey, what—"

I didn't give him a chance to ask the question. I hoofed it into the bathroom, locked the door, and held my breath. I couldn't hear anything, and I cursed the solid door, but eventually, after a long silence, I heard the door to the room close.

After letting out the breath I'd been holding, I took a piss, and then headed into the shower.

Serves you right.

Thinking there might be something.

With a guy you barely knew.

Yet when I returned to the room, and the smell of sex hit me, I found I couldn't regret what I'd done. Harold had made me feel alive. Forced me to connect with someone, if only for a short time.

I was grateful the room had two queen beds, so I didn't have to lie in our spunk-filled love nest.

Jesus.

As I went to strip the bed, I found a note on the pillow.

When you're ready to stop running, you know where to find me.

Of all the arrogant... Yet I couldn't bring myself to throw out the note. Maybe I could have a friend. I didn't do cheating, but maybe...did I want to be friends with someone who took sex so casually?

Except it hadn't felt casual. It'd been the opposite of casual.

Damn.

I dropped onto the bed in defeat. I wasn't going to sleep on the fresh bed. I was going to sleep enveloped in his scent. I was going to dream of him, and the life we might've had.

Chapter Four

Derek

I'm a fool.

I called myself that about a million times before I showed up at the hockey rink early Sunday morning.

I'd dressed up Saturday night, planning to go over to Ace's Place and give the bartender a piece of my mind. Except he didn't deserve that. I might get him fired, and what would that accomplish? I wasn't vindictive, even if he hurt me.

After sleeping another night in those sheets—because I hadn't let housekeeping take them away, and wasn't that sentimentality gone overboard—I awoke this morning, knowing what I had to do.

Yesterday I'd gone to the superstore and loaded up on winter supplies. Vancouver might dip below freezing a few days a year, and we had the occasional snowfall, but nothing like these mountains. The Coquihalla Pass was often shut down because of snow, and accidents were common up this way. Well, if I was going to be a permanent resident, I had to dress the part. The cashier eyed me, I'm sure wondering what the fuck I was doing, but she happily rang up my purchases that almost hit four figures. My hotel room was full of supplies, just ready to head over to my new home. I'd debated renting but had gotten a sweet deal on a house. A real house. Like the one my grandparents had owned. Since real estate was rarely a bad bet, I took the plunge.

Now, as I spent more time in town, I was seeing things weren't so bad. Several big box retail stores. Numerous restaurants.

One awesome sports bar.

The snow was falling lightly when I exited my brand-new SUV. I hadn't even owned a car in Vancouver, but my grandmother insisted I learn how to drive. I occasionally rented a car to go up to Whistler for a ski vacation, but I tended to stick close to home. I had everything I needed in the city, so why go elsewhere? How narrow-minded. An entire world existed beyond the city, and I'd never seen it. I thought myself better than everyone else.

You were wrong.

By the time I entered the arena, a light dusting of snow covered the area. As I brushed it off, a woman passed me. "You here for the game?"

The sound of blades across the ice caught my attention.

I met her gaze. "Yeah, I think so."

"Well, grab a coffee and come sit with me." She pointed to a nearby bleacher.

Small-town friendly?

What did I have to lose? I got a cup of coffee and joined the woman and her friend.

Even before I settled, she stuck out her hand. "I'm Tamara, and this is my friend Twyla."

The other woman held up a gloved hand.

"I'm with Micah, and Twyla here is with Neil." She gave me the once-over. "Who are you with?"

"Uh..." I hadn't really thought this through. "Well, West invited me. And I know Harold."

"Harold...?"

Twyla snickered. "Only Ace's mother calls him Harold." She eyed me speculatively. "Unless he's trying to impress someone."

"Or hide the fact he owns Ace's Place," Tamara chimed in. Her pale eyes settled on me. "Welcome. He's been alone a long time."

"Well, he has Benjamin." I didn't want them to think I was a home-wrecker.

Both women broke into peals of laughter. Laughter that went on so long, I wondered if I should just get up and leave.

Tamara placed a hand on my thigh.

A little forward, but I got the feeling she didn't mean it unkindly.

"Benjamin is his eighty-pound Bouvier. The pooch is two-years-old and afraid of his own shadow. Ace is mighty protective of that little guy."

Little? Eighty pounds?

"And defensive." Twyla's contribution. Her short dark curls bounced as she nodded. "You'd better like dogs."

I didn't not like dogs. I didn't do dogs. I supposed that would change.

If Harold, wait—Ace, wanted me. Now I reflected, West hadn't been all that comfortable using the name Harold either.

"I'm not sure I'm good enough for him."

Tamara's amusement fled. "You're here, aren't you? Not many guys show up at this early hour on a Sunday morning to watch a bunch of men play pick-up hockey. Ace and West have to play on opposing teams because together they'd slaughter the competition. See, this is all for fun. That being said, the men take this seriously." She pointed out across the ice. "My Micah is the goalie. This is his bonding time with the guys. He works in the sawmill, and that's a great union job, but it doesn't do much for his spirit. Being here does."

I'd certainly never viewed a sport that way. Not my thing, but I'd try. If freezing my ass off every Sunday morning meant I had a shot, I'd give it my all.

"Always bring a foam seat to sit on and a blanket to put over your lap. Trust me, you won't feel stupid after the first time." Tamara winked.

Twyla yelled something, and both women rose to their feet, cheering. Since I had no idea either what'd happened or whose team Ace was on, I stayed seated. The men all had their names on the backs of their jerseys, but I didn't actually know Ace's last name.

Turns out I knew very little about him.

"Oh, in case you're wondering, number thirty-two is Catherine. Don't let her gender fool you, she can dish it out and take it."

I spotted the woman in question and yes, she was slightly smaller than the other men. But size was relative. They all looked huge in the bulky hockey equipment.

The ref blew the whistle, and my two new friends cheered. Tamara patted me on the shoulder as the men headed for the benches.

"Ace's team won. By a whopping one goal. Micah's going to be pleased no one scored on him today." She folded up her blanket and stomped her feet a few times. "No matter how many socks I wear, my feet are always blocks of ice."

"I told you to use the foot warmers." Twyla also rose and folded her blanket. "Neil's team lost, but he won't care."

I followed the two women as they walked to the end of the row and descended to the main floor. Nerves set in as I absorbed the fact

I was really here. This was it. He might reject me. I'd treated him abominably, and he might decide I wasn't worth the effort.

First Twyla squealed in delight as a man approached. She ruffled his damp hair and gave him a huge kiss. He snagged her by the waist and pulled her close. "I love that you're as enthusiastic when I lose as when I win."

"Because you'll always be a winner to me."

Pure sap. And a few months ago, I might've gagged. Now I saw it for what it was—affection and love.

Tamara patted me on the back and moved to greet the next player. He dropped his bag, grabbed her by the waist, and hoisted her up. She laughed with glee as he spun her around.

"I was awesome, wasn't I?"

"Baby, you're always great." She gave him a long look, and as she slid down his body, he looked at me, cocking his head.

"And you are...?"

West slapped Micah on the back. "He's here for me."

Micah cackled. There was no other word for it.

"I think he might be here for me."

Ace spoke the words softly, but as Micah stepped back and away, Ace's gaze met mine.

Words caught in my throat. Could I do this? Was I prepared to make a public declaration?

"I *might* be here for you. Harold."

West guffawed, and everyone else broke into laughter. Several more players had joined our little group, and clearly this was an ongoing joke.

"It's, uh, Ace."

"I know. What I don't know is why you didn't tell me the truth."

He looked down and scuffed his boot on the cement floor.

"Because Ace is a pretty big deal in town, and he wanted you to get to know him before you discovered that." West ran his hand through his damp hair.

Harold...Ace... Whoever. Two points of color rose in his already flushed cheeks, but he finally met my gaze. His eyes blazed.

"We, uh, usually go to A&W for breakfast." He hiked his bag higher on his shoulder.

Was that an invitation?

Twyla swatted him. "Derek can join us next week, right?" Her eyes shone brightly. "I think you guys need to go somewhere to talk."

I gulped. She was right, of course, we needed to talk. Who knew if there was even going to be a next weekend? Ace hadn't actually said it was okay that I'd ventured here today.

"Talk. Yeah." Ace glanced over at his teammates who were all moving toward the exit. The next group of hockey players were making their way onto the ice, and the stands were filing. This group was much younger, so the spectators were parents and grandparents and a few siblings thrown in for good measure. I was so out of my comfort zone.

Ace ran his hand through his hair. "I desperately need a shower."

I almost offered to join him but figured that'd be just a bit too forward.

"Would you..." He scrubbed a hand down his face, drawing attention to the scruff. God, scruff was so fucking sexy. "Would you want to come home with me? To talk," he was quick to add.

"Why don't I do drive-thru A&W and meet you at your place? That way you can shower, and I can feed you." Nothing to be gained by tiptoeing around the situation.

His grin was wide, showing off perfect teeth. Impressive for a guy who played contact sports. He furtively glanced around. I knew what he was doing, so remained still. In two strides he was before me. I expected the kiss, but it still threw me a bit. Quick and light.

He rattled off an address and was out the door before I had a chance to get my bearings.

I hadn't even asked him what he wanted to eat.

Chapter Five

Derek

I figured four breakfast sandwiches and a pile of hash browns between the two of us would suffice. I added coffees and OJ as well,
not wanting to assume what he had in his fridge. As I drove to his
house, with the help of GPS, I reflected on how little I knew about
him. His friends obviously adored him. Admired him. That kind of
esteem wasn't easy to earn. His humbleness surprised me, though. He
could've been boastful Friday night. Instead, he'd kept quiet about
who he was and what he'd accomplished.

The house was an unassuming rancher at the end of a cul-de-sac.
I parked on the street and looked around the neighborhood. Nice
houses. Nice lawns. Even beneath the snow, I could see everything
was well-tended. Very...suburban. Closer to what I'd grown up in than
what I'd been used to in recent years. I grabbed the bag of food and
balanced the drink tray while I locked the door to my SUV. Something
told me I could probably leave it unlocked. This neighborhood had

that kind of vibe. City paranoia was ingrained, though, so I locked it and set the alarm.

The driveway led to a path which, in turn, led to the front door.

A note was taped.

Come on in. Make yourself at home.

Ah, so my instincts about this being a safe area were confirmed. Not sure I'd have ever left my front door open—even if I had someone coming over. I balanced the food on the drinks and opened the door. I toed off my boots in the entryway and wandered into the house. The warmth assailed me, as did the gentle woodsy smell from the fireplace. Cute. He'd started a fire. Was that a practical gesture or a romantic one? I wasn't sure.

I walked toward the back of the house, easily locating the kitchen. I put the food and drinks on the counter and made my way over to the sliding glass door. Was I snooping? Yep. Did I want to know more about this man and his home? Absolutely. I shucked off my coat and hung it on the back of a kitchen chair before looking outside.

The view brought me up short.

Stunning.

I saw the back deck, and from there an unobstructed view of what I assumed was all the Nicola Valley. The mountains on the far side down to the entire town of Merritt. A view similar to this would cost a fortune in Vancouver, and I idly wondered what he'd paid for it.

Something butted my knee, and I looked down in surprise to see the cutest black dog looking up at me with soulful chocolate-brown eyes. The dog came nearly to my waist.

"Well, hello Benjamin."

He cocked his head, clearly surprised.

"Oh, I've heard about you. You're quite famous."

The dog nuzzled my hand and I petted his soft curly fur. I pulled back, but he butted my hip. I had to shift so as to not get knocked over. Man, this dog was strong.

"He'll insist you pet him until your arm gets tired." Ace whistled and, after an endless moment, Benjamin backed away from me.

"He's adorable."

"And he knows it."

I turned to face Ace just as he came up to me.

"I didn't kiss you properly earlier." He took my cheeks in his hands and leaned in for a kiss. This one was not light and sweet. He thrust his tongue into my mouth, and I moaned at the contact. He yanked me closer until our bodies pressed together. He wore sweatpants and a hoodie, so when he came flush with me, his erection rubbed against my denim-clad hip. He ran his hands through my hair, using the leverage to pull us even closer.

His fresh-soap smell invaded my senses, kicking my libido into high gear. God, I wanted him with a ferocity and passion I wasn't accustomed to. Guys before? I could take'em or leave'em. But this man? I wanted to possess. To be possessed.

He pulled back and met my gaze. His eyes were unfocused, his cheeks pink, a sheen of sweat across his brow, and his lips were kiss-swollen. Debauched.

His nose twitched. "As much as I want to eat you right now, I need food."

I grinned. "Well, I brought food. Two bacon sandwiches, two sausage, and a pile of hash browns." I hesitated. "I hope you're not a vegetarian." There'd been several items on his menu.

"Nah, meat eater all the way. Do I feel guilty? You bet. Does it stop me? Oh hell, no." He pulled back from me and stepped to the counter. Benjamin also stuck his nose in the air. "No." Ace's growl was clear, and although the dog hesitated, he did eventually back off and head to a bed in the corner of the room.

Ace pulled out all the food and spread it on the counter. He motioned for me to pick. I snagged the bacon, but before I could do anything, he snatched it from me. He headed over to the microwave where he tossed it in. "Lukewarm is no good. Got to be piping hot." When the machine dinged, he removed the sandwich and handed it to me.

Sheesh, he wasn't kidding. The wrapper was so hot I could barely hold it.

He dumped the hash browns on a plate and put them in next. He glanced at me and then indicated the kitchen table.

Obediently, I sat. While my food cooled, I watched him with eager admiration. He moved with the same fluid grace I'd seen at the bar. For such a big guy, he was light on his feet.

He put the juice on the table and then heated the coffees. "Don't wait for me."

Another devastating grin. My stomach did a little flip. "I'm waiting for it to cool."

An arched eyebrow. "Ah, I'll note that for next time. I take my coffee extra hot."

And I preferred slightly cooled.

He placed the plate of hash browns on the table, added our coffees, then put his sandwiches in front of him as he sat.

He glanced at me, and I indicated he should eat.

Eat? More like inhale. He wasn't rude, but he downed those three sandwiches and half the hash browns before I finished my sandwich. I grinned in amusement.

After wiping his mouth, he took a long gulp of coffee. Finally, he sighed and leaned back, patting his flat stomach. "That was amazing. Thank you."

I waved my hand. "I didn't do anything." I spun my coffee cup ninety degrees. "I mean, you missed going out with your friends." Another ninety-degree spin.

Ace grasped my hand, stilling me. His fingers wrapped over mine, and he squeezed. "I love my friends, but I see them every weekend during the hockey season. We also play softball in the summer. And a few of us play two-on-two basketball, and several of them play golf." He shuddered.

I smiled. "Not a golf fan?"

"Uh, hitting a little ball with a piece of metal and trying to get it into a little hole? No, not my idea of fun."

His charming grin was wide. I melted every time he bestowed that smile upon me.

"What would you like to do?"

I wondered if he meant sex, but I wasn't ready for that yet. I pointed to the deck. "I want you to show me your view first."

He cocked an eyebrow. "Oh, yeah, that I can do." He rose and snagged the plates. He put them in the sink and then tossed out the wrappers. "You might want to get your boots."

After eyeing the snow on the deck, I agreed with that sentiment. I walked back to the front door and snagged them. When I got back to the sliding glass door, I put them on. "Do I need my coat?"

He waved me off. "Nah, I don't plan to keep you out for long. And then we can head into the living room. I've got a fire going."

"Trying to woo me?"

"Any chance?"

"I might be persuaded." I hadn't come for sex—or for anything else for that matter—but a little nookie? Yeah, I was up for that.

He unlatched the lock and slid the door back. A blast of cold air hit me, and I stepped out quickly. He joined me, sidestepping the enthusiastic dog barrelling out, and then slid the door closed.

"Keeping in the heat."

Benjamin promptly ran down the stairs into the yard where the snow was several feet deep.

He sank nearly to his shoulders, and when he looked back, I could've sworn he had a grin on this face. I moved to the edge of the balcony and felt the same sense of wonder. The view was stunning. Strong arms banded around me as a warm chest pressed against my cooling back.

"You're even more amazing than the view." He whispered the words in my ear, his breath tickling my neck.

"Bullshit." The response erupted from me.

His grip tightened. "Nope. Ace doesn't bullshit. He's a straight shooter. And he's telling you that you're not only sexy as fuck, but one of the good guys. You did the right thing, and if that led you to me, then I'm the lucky one."

Warmth suffused me despite the chill in the air. I'd never believed in fate. One made their own destiny by making carefully considered choices. The move to Merritt, visiting Ace's Place, going to the game this morning—these were all things I'd never have done six months ago. Decisions I'd never have made.

Yet they all felt perfectly correct now.

Ace bit my earlobe and a shiver ran through me. Funny, I only saw him as Ace now. Harold was just the name his mother used. When he tugged me back toward the door, I took one last look around. As

I did, the clouds parted, and a beam of sunlight cut across the valley. Stunning.

Once I was back in the house, I removed my boots and placed them on a rubber mat. Ace did the same, and he petted Benjamin when the dog bounded in, covered in snow. Must have been playing in the stuff.

Would I ever get used to the sheer volume of it? Possibly. Probably. Didn't have much of a choice. "I, uh, need to borrow your bathroom."

He gave me a quick grin and pointed down the hall. "Second door on your right."

I found myself in a modern four-piece bathroom. White with slate gray accents. The entire house felt both modern and traditional. Although I needed to piss, I also needed a moment to center myself. I was about to have a conversation that was going to be pithy and light or that might determine my future. A lot of pressure to put on one little discussion. I washed my hands and did a quick check in the mirror.

You can do this.

I walked down the hall and into the family room.

Benjamin lay on a rug in front of the wood-burning fireplace. A massive sectional couch dominated the room with recliners on either side of it, and all seats faced a big-screen television. A comfortable place to hang out with the guys and watch a game.

Or a good place to Netflix and chill?

I gulped.

Ace sat on the sectional and patted the space next to him. The space was even warmer now than before. I yanked my sweatshirt over my head and felt the instant relief as my bare arms hit the air. I tossed the hoodie onto one of the recliners and took up the seat Ace suggested. We faced the fireplace and the smell again enveloped me. Not familiar, and yet not strange. Something I suspected I could get used to.

"Wood burning isn't good for the environment, so I usually use my gas fireplace. I only trot out wood for special occasions."

Okay, well, pretty blunt.

"I appreciate it. I like the rustic feel." I swept my hand to encompass the place. "You have a lovely home."

No mistaking the pride shining in his dark-brown eyes, or the grin. "When I bought the property, it had an old starter home that'd seen better days. But that view? Deserved a home to match. We tore everything down and built this one with all the modern amenities. Oh." He smiled lasciviously. "You should see the soaker tub in the master bathroom. And the view."

"You'll just have to show me."

"I can give you the tour right now."

He started to rise, but I placed a hand on his thigh.

"Maybe in a bit." Because if we didn't get through the chit-chat and on to the main conversation soon, I might've lost my nerve.

A look crossed his face. "Yeah, okay." He resettled. "You want to know why I didn't tell you the truth."

I shook my head. "Nah, your friends explained that pretty clearly. Did I feel stupid when Twyla and Tamara were laughing? Yeah, a little bit. But I knew they weren't laughing at me or being unkind. Just laughing at your antics."

Relief washed across his face and he rubbed his hand up and down it. "Yeah, I meant to tell you. I was planning to as I was getting dressed, but then you tossed me out—"

"Yeah, about that—"

"—and on the way home it dawned on me you didn't know who Benjamin was and, of course, it sounded like I was cheating. Which I'd never do. And I almost drove back except I didn't have the key card and

Benjamin was waiting and..." He scratched his stubble. "I just hoped you'd show up again. If not, I planned on tracking you down."

That caught my attention.

"You did?"

He snagged my left hand, enveloping it in his two massive ones. "Yeah, for sure. I mean, maybe you don't feel the way I do...but Friday night was special. For me. And I hope for you too, but that's incredibly presumptuous of me."

"And yet if the feeling is reciprocated, then it's just you being brave and speaking out first."

"Huh." A frown marred his brow.

I pressed my thumb between his eyebrows. "Don't overthink it. We had a good time. We connected. Maybe we're both looking for more, or maybe this'll just be great sex that fizzles out."

"No fizzle. There will be no fizzling. Only sizzle. Plenty of sizzling."

His vehemence brought a smile to my face. He was quite adamant about this. His optimism was infectious, and I found myself running through scenarios in my mind. "So, we're going to keep seeing each other."

"Oh, hell yes, we are." He squeezed my hand almost to the point of pain. "I'm not letting you go without a fight."

He barely had me and he already felt this strongly? Something warmed me from within.

He released my hand then cupped my cheeks. "You're worth fighting for."

The intensity in his eyes stole my breath and the back of my eyes prickled. How often over the past six months had I questioned my worth? How many times had I wondered if I made the right decision, turning in colleagues who trusted me? How frequently had I fought the urge to give up the fight?

"I am worth it." And I meant it. To this man, I had true value. And I suspected some new friends as well.

"Can I kiss you now?"

He felt he needed to ask? Something in that considerate gesture reassured. Comforted. "I'd love it."

I moved forward as he did, and just before our lips pressed together, he grinned. His soft lips pressed to mine, and I nipped his bottom lip. He opened his mouth, and I thrust my tongue in, demanding admittance. I wasn't sure if this was a reverential sealing of a promise, or the beginning of something physical. Something demanding.

It didn't matter. We had all the time in the world. And as he ran his hands through my hair, my desire kicked into high gear and my cock strained against my jeans. I wanted this. Whatever this was. Whatever he was offering, I'd happily take it.

Right until a furry head poked between the two of us and we broke apart.

Benjamin placed his massive head on Ace's thigh and gazed up between the two of us.

Ace sighed.

"He doesn't like competition for your attention?"

A shrug. "Actually, I've never brought anyone home."

"In two years?" I couldn't keep the teasing from my voice.

His eyes sharpened. "I didn't say I was celibate..." He snickered. "But pretty much. He's been my sole focus, and apparently he's a little spoiled." He glared at the dog who simply grinned, tongue lolling. "We could, uh, take this into the bedroom."

I petted Benjamin on the head. "Nah. We've got all the time in the world. Why not let him get comfortable with me first?"

Again, relief washed over Ace. Relief that I understood? I might not have much experience with dogs, but I knew how I'd feel if my person started paying rapt attention to someone else. If that meant we split our attention for now, I was good with that.

Ace angled himself against the corner of the couch and reclined, tugging me with him. Benjamin, apparently sensing the change in mood, headed back for his blanket. I let Ace pull me to him. I laid my head on his muscular chest and accepted the comfort he offered as he wrapped his arm around me shoulder.

How long we lay like that, I wasn't sure. I was accustomed to doing the deed and heading out, but I wasn't in any hurry. And even if we did nothing today, I was okay with that too. Just being here — just being held by him — that was all I could ask for. I didn't know what the future for us held, but I could feel the promise. Sense the possibility.

Too little time had passed for me to know my true feelings, but the rightness pervaded my bones and sank into my soul.

I never wanted to leave.

Epilogue

Zach slammed me into the boards, and I grunted. He wasn't as powerful as West, but he could do serious damage. All for fun meant most of the time we took it easy, but his team was down by one goal and the clock was running out. I shot the puck wildly and, to my dread, West picked it off. He snapped his wrist and Micah didn't stand a chance.

The buzzer sounded.

West, Zach, Neil, and the rest of their team exploded with glee. Twyla and Tamara could be heard clear across the ice.

So could Derek.

A tie.

A pretty decent way to end the season. We didn't do shoot-outs, so the game was called. My team had won the season by two games, so that was something. All in fun was great, but I appreciated bragging rights. Come September all bets were off.

West slapped my back as we skated over to the boards. "I think you have the loudest cheering section."

He wasn't wrong.

I turned to Zach. "Did I see you driving a Mini Cooper?"

"My sister Anika's car. She needed my SUV to haul around some class supplies." He scratched his nose. "I don't enjoy doing the pass in the car, but the roads are clear and we've had an early spring. Keeping my eye on the forecast, though."

Zach adored his much-younger sister. West let it slip once that Zach had another sister. She'd died in a car crash over ten years ago. A death Zach never recovered from.

I couldn't imagine that kind of anguish. My sisters were pains in my ass, but I loved them like crazy, and couldn't imagine life without them.

In the dressing room we quickly shed our gear and loaded up our bags. I pulled on jeans and a hoodie from the community college. The hoodie Derek gave me for Christmas. To remind me to whom I belonged.

As if I could ever forget.

He'd stepped into my bar just over a year ago, and my life had changed completely.

I stuck my hand in my pocket to make sure I hadn't forgotten anything.

West nudged me. "You sure you want an audience?"

Was I? I'd vacillated between epic and intimate. Finally I settled on A&W on a Sunday morning with the gang. It felt...right. This group had welcomed Derek into their fold, and more than a few times he'd joined the wives and girlfriends for activities. He wasn't big on gender roles, and his support of me was absolute. Adorable.

Plus, we were celebrating the end of the trial in Vancouver. Guilty. The whole lot of them. I worried Derek might use that victory to parlay an entry back into the Vancouver business community, but he made it clear he loved teaching and he wasn't looking back. No, he kept looking forward.

"I think so."

West grinned. Then it dipped a bit. As it always did. He didn't think anyone saw, but I did. He was meant for permanence and a relationship. His ill-conceived marriage to Sylvia was long in the rearview mirror but he still ached. Whether for her, or someone else, I didn't know.

Catherine smacked me upside the head. "Don't overthink it. Go with your instinct. If it doesn't feel right, wait until it does. Derek's not going anywhere."

She had a good point.

En masse we trudged to the waiting group. Tamara was there first to throw herself at Micah. "I love you, even if you let that goal sneak past you." She punched West on the shoulder. "Nice shot."

He shrugged. "Lucky shot."

But it hadn't been. West was fucking talented. A shame he hadn't made it to the NHL, but if that meant we got to own him here in Merritt, then we were the lucky ones. Twyla pounced on Neil and I caught a wistful expression in Zach's face. West had intimated there were a few women but nothing stuck. Our two most attractive men were also our two bachelors.

Derek stepped around the group and approached me. I cocked my head at his look of discomfort. Had someone said something to him?

Was he okay? I placed my bag on the ground and was about to reach for him when he dropped to one knee.

Oh, holy hell.

"I just..." He cleared his throat. "It's been a year and I can't see myself living without you." He swept his hand to indicate the group. "They're your family, and I wanted them to be here for this. I mean, your mom and your sisters are your family as well, and of course I wish they were here too, and maybe—"

"Oh for fuck's sake, just ask him." Tamara's voice wasn't unkind, but she laced it with frustration.

"Yeah, uh, okay." He held out a ring. "Will you marry me? Be mine?"

Words escaped me, but I dug into my pocket and pulled out the ring I'd intended to give him later. His eyes lit and his grin was wry.

"Great minds." His words, my sentiment.

I held out my hand, and he took it, allowing me to haul him up. He wrapped his arms around my neck and pulled me down for a kiss. A hard kiss. A demanding kiss. An *I want everything* kiss.

Hoots and hollers erupted from our friends.

Derek pulled back with a huge grin on his face. He held out the ring, and I presented my left hand. The fit was a little tight over the knuckle, but I didn't intend to ever take it off.

I held his hand and, to my infinite relief, the ring fit. I brought his hand to my lips and pressed a reverential kiss to the ring. "Forever."

He blinked several times. "Yeah, forever."

I cleared my throat. "Now, will you *finally* move in with me? Benjamin wishes you didn't have to go home so often." I'd been dropping hints for more than six months, but he always had one excuse or another. All flimsy, as far as I was concerned.

"He signed the papers yesterday. The house goes on the market tomorrow." Catherine grinned.

As she was the top realtor in town, hardly a surprise Derek chose her. She'd get him a good price, and he'd have a comfortable nest egg. Since I owned my place and the bar outright, we were in good shape.

Of course, if he had nothing but the clothes on his back, I'd take him just as fast.

Tamara broke the moment by launching herself into Derek's arms and West slapped me on the back. Twyla hugged Derek as, in turn, Zach, Neil, Micah, and the rest of the team shook my hand or patted me on the back. Catherine—gruff Catherine—gave me a hug and an extra-hard squeeze.

"Don't fuck this up."

I chuckled. "I don't intend to."

After the gang had offered all the congratulations, I gave up my ultimate secret. "Elissa is manning the kitchen and Upton is manning the bar, so everyone's invited back to my place."

West encompassed the group in a sweeping gesture. "I'm assuming you mean Ace's Place and not your house."

Shit.

"Uh, yeah, you would be correct." As lovely as my house was, it couldn't hold twenty-five people. Summers when we were in the backyard? Sure. Dead of winter? Not a chance.

Derek tucked himself into my side and pressed a kiss to my cheek. "I know I say this every day, but I really love you. Moving here was the best decision I have ever made."

"Well, right up there with giving me your key card."

West hooted. Yeah, pretty much everyone knew the story by now. How our hook-up at Ace's Place had become our forever.

Forever.

I couldn't be happier.

Enjoying your visit to Mission City? Why not check out the entire series?
Grab Maddox and Ravi's story here!
Ginger Snapping All the Way (Love in Mission City Book 1)

Also available:
Ginger Snapping All the Way (Love in Mission City Book 1)
Stanley's Christmas Redemption (Love in Mission City Book 2)
The Beauty of the Beast (Love in Mission City Book 2.5)
Sleigh Bells and Second Chances (Love in Mission City Book 3)
A Daddy for Christmas 2: Foster(Love in Mission City Book 3.5)
Rayne's Return (Love in Mission City Book 4)
Love in Mission City: The Boyfriends Duet
Love in Mission City: The Shorts
Puppy Pride
Rayne Check
Archer's Awakening
Thought You Were the One
Love Without Reservations
Also
Axe to Grind
Grindstone's Edge
Hugh (Single Dads of Gaynor Beach)
Anthony (Single Dads of Gaynor Beach)
Xavier (Single Dads of Gaynor Beach)

Love Furever (Friends of Gaynor Beach Animal Rescue)
Husky Love(Friends of Gaynor Beach Animal Rescue)
Yorkie to My Heart (Friends of Gaynor Beach Animal Rescue)
My Past, Your Future
If Only for Today
Catch a Tiger by the Tail
Solstice Surprise
Valentino in Vancouver
You See Me
Sun, Surf, and Surprises
An Uncommon Gentleman
A Sensible Gentleman
Sizzling Sydney Nights
Caressa's Homecoming (Bound by LoveBook 1)
Cole's Reckoning (Bound by Love Book 2)
Didn't See You Coming
Finding Noah (Foggy Basin Season 2)

Audiobooks
Ginger Snapping All the Way
Stanley's Christmas Redemption
Sleigh Bells and Second Chances
Love in Mission City: The Shorts
Page Against the Machine
The Lightkeeper's Love Affair
Ace's Place
Marcus's Cadence
Not in it for the Money

Hugh (Single Dads of Gaynor Beach)

Anthony (Single Dads of Gaynor Beach)

Love Furever (Friends of Gaynor Beach Animal Rescue)

My Past, Your Future

If Only for Today

Catch a Tiger by the Tail

Solstice Surprise

An Uncommon Gentleman

A Sensible Gentleman

Didn't See You Coming

Want a free short story? The story is set in Gaynor Beach, California where there are plenty of single dads and puppy rescues! You can sign up for my newsletter so you can keep up with all the great stuff I'm doing as well as pictures of my own pooches, Ally and Finnegan.

Hemingway's Happy Day

Love contemporary MF romances? What's better than love in the beautiful Cedar Valley in British Columbia, Canada? Find small town romances with a touch of angst, a bit of heat, and a lot of heart...

The Absolution of Abigail Reardon(prequel)

The Luminosity of LorianaHarper (Book 1)

The Making of Marnie Jones(Book 2)

The Redemption of RemySt. Claire (Book 3)

Interested in knowing more about Gabbi?

Sign up for her newsletter
Follow her on Bookbub
Follow her on Instagram

USA Today Bestselling author Gabbi Grey lives in beautiful British Columbia where her fur baby chin-poo keeps her safe from the nasty neighborhood squirrels. Working for the government by day, she spends her early mornings writing contemporary, gay, sweet, and dark erotic BDSM romances. While she firmly believes in happy endings, she also believes in making her characters suffer before finding their true love. She also writes m/f romances as Gabbi Black and Gabbi Powell.

www.ingramcontent.com/pod-product-compliance
Lightning Source LLC
Chambersburg PA
CBHW031611240626
47153CB00002B/711